Dear Romance Reader,

Welcome to a world of breathtaking passion and never-ending romance.
Welcome to *Precious Gem Romances*.

It is our pleasure to present *Precious Gem Romances,* a wonderful new line of romance books by some of America's best-loved authors. Let these thrilling historical and contemporary romances sweep you away to far-off times and places in stories that will dazzle your senses and melt your heart.

Sparkling with joy, laughter, and love, each *Precious Gem Romance* glows with all the passion and excitement you expect from the very best in romance. Offered at a great affordable price, these books are an irresistible value—and an essential addition to your romance collection. Tender love stories you will want to read again and again, *Precious Gem Romances* are books you will treasure forever.

Look for fabulous new *Precious Gem Romances* each month—available only at Wal★Mart.

Kate Duffy
Editorial Director

IT'S IN
HIS KISS

DEBORAH SHELLEY

Zebra Books
Kensington Publishing Corp.
http://www.zebrabooks.com

*To our parents, Jennie and Billy Burrell
and Mary and Tom Mitchell, with love*

ONE

"Okay, so where's the rest of it?" Dangling the leopard-print thong panties between her finger and thumb, Jacqueline Santiago raised her eyebrow at Mia Alvarez, her young cousin.

"You're holding it."

It was bad enough having a dozen of her closest friends show up on her doorstep for a surprise wedding shower, but the theme of the shower, "Simply Steamy," almost did her in. Jacki sighed as she returned the thong to its tasteless, erotically decorated box, quickly closing the equally suggestive lid.

The giggling guests peeked into the box as they passed it around, and hooted as Mia tried to explain her choice of gifts. "You know you're my favorite female cousin, Jacki . . ." Successfully avoiding eye contact, Mia looked instead at the ceiling fan spinning above their heads in the spacious living room of the home they shared.

Jacki gritted her teeth and prayed for patience. "I'm your only female cousin.

"Right. *And* my favorite. But . . ."

"But what?" Jacki waited for an interesting, if not creative response.

Mia gestured dramatically. "But here you are, ready to be married in a couple of days to old what's-his-name, but where's the romance? You don't feel passion for him in your soul." She turned to the woman sitting beside her and shrugged. "In fact, I don't think the man even has a soul."

Jacki groaned. Mia meant well, but had never outgrown the habit of saying exactly what she thought at the very moment she thought it. Jacki steeled herself as she reminded Mia, "Evan. His name is Evan."

"Evan. Yeah, that's right. Evan. You've been engaged to him for two years now . . ."

"A year and a half."

"A year and a half. And I've never seen him kiss you. Not even a good-bye peck on the cheek, let alone a pucker-'em-up, face-sucking smooch. You guys don't even hold hands."

"And that," Jacki pointed at the present, which was still being passed among the women seated in a makeshift circle of assorted chairs and ottomans, "will make us hold hands?"

Grabbing a handful of salted tortilla chips from a nearby basket, Mia munched thoughtfully before answering. "I hope to heaven it does more than that."

Jacki sat down next to Mia and handed her a napkin when she started licking the oil and salt from her fingers.

Mia crumpled it and returned it to her. "I mean it. You two need all the help you can get. Romantically speaking, that is. Evan is about as exciting as a wilted head of lettuce. I know he's the opposite of those sexy dudes you used to go for, but for the life of me, I still can't figure out why you'd prefer polyester over leather."

Leaping to her fiancé's defense, especially in light of the fact every woman in the room had met him, Jacki protested, "Now that I've turned thirty, I don't have time for those hormonal-based attractions. Evan and I have a relationship based on friendship and trust and respect for each other. He's just not . . . demonstrative," she added weakly.

"Look at yourself, cuz. A tall, gorgeous woman like you is 'way too good for that *pescado muy frio.*"

"Cold fish," Jacki translated for the woman next to her, who immediately burst into embarrassed laughter.

"*Very* cold fish," Mia corrected. "You deserve a love so strong, so passionate, so overwhelming, that your toes will curl up just looking at him."

"You've been reading too many of those romances, *prima,*" Jacki sighed.

"No way. There's no such thing as reading too many romances. Besides, you're never going to see me with some stick-in-the-mud. Now the one before Fish Face—who was that, Roc?—he showed a lot of potential."

"Roc did look awfully fine on his Harley," one of her other friends commented, batting her eyelashes at the memory.

"I still can't see how you went from the wild side to the mild side," Mia snapped her fingers, "just like that."

"First of all, Evan is very dependable. He has a stable personality, and a highly developed sense of responsibility."

Ignoring her cousin's doubtful expression, Jacki continued, "Unlike Roc, Evan's incapable of lying. And he keeps his promises. Just the other day . . ."

The persistent ringing of the phone interrupted her praises. "Let the machine pick it up," Jacki said, passing around a bowl of spicy pistachio nuts.

Silence fell over the room as the women chewed on the nuts. Jacki knew darned well they were only pretending not to listen.

"Jacqueline, this is Evan Snow, your fiancé."

Mia snorted. "He has to remind you? He must be afraid you'd forget."

"I'm sorry I didn't call you right away, but I just wanted you to know I made it safely to my conference in Las Vegas," his voice droned on.

"He's very good about checking in with me," Jacki smiled, picking up a plastic glass full of sangria punch.

"You wouldn't believe what a rough flight we had. By the time we got to the hotel, Allison had become extremely nauseous."

"Who's Allison?" someone whispered.

Quietly, Jacki responded, "His business partner."

Evan's voice became softer. "Then she told me it wasn't the plane ride that made her sick to her stomach. She's been, uh, ill like this every morning for the last month."

There was a long pause. Someone coughed nervously.

The voice on the tape began to speak faster. "Mmm, Jacqueline, it's extremely difficult for me to tell you this, but Allison's morning sickness is my fault. So you see, I had no choice but to marry her.

The wedding took place about an hour ago. I hope it isn't too late for you to return our wedding presents and get your deposit back on the reception hall. Anyway, I'm sorry to have missed you. Have a nice evening."

The shower party became so quiet Jacki could have heard a ball of cotton crash to the floor. With every eye in the room on her, she sat motionless at the end of the sofa, too mortified to move. Several minutes passed before she set down her glass.

Taking a napkin to wipe an imaginary spill off the coffee table, she looked down as she spoke. "See, Mia, you were very wrong. Evan *can* feel passion. The problem is—none of it's for me."

"So much for Mr. Respectability," Mia philosophized as she reached for the dish of pastel mints.

Patrick Godwin swore softly under his breath as the battered minivan in front of him pulled into the last empty spot in the multi-storied concrete parking structure. He whipped his metallic gray rental car around and drove down the exit ramp three times as fast as the posted speed limit.

The actual exit came up more quickly than he'd anticipated. Slamming on his brakes, he came to an abrupt stop, staring in wonder at the long lines of traffic in both directions blocking his path from the parking garage to the main street.

Moments later, he pulled in front of a man who had the bad luck to be driving just slightly slower than the rest of the cars on the crowded road. Shrugging apologetically in the general direction of the honks and shouts and screeches of brakes, he resumed his search for a parking space. After another ten minutes of driving up and down the streets of downtown Phoenix, Patrick finally found a place at the curb a little over five blocks away from the Goldwater Centre.

Opening the car door, the heat felt just as bad as he remembered from the walk across the rental lot at the airport. Patrick shrugged out of his jacket, picked up his blueprints and closed the car door. As he turned to the parking meter, he fumbled through his pockets for change, and found two quarters.

As he continued the fruitless search for more quarters in his other pockets, the blueprints slipped. Making a wild, futile grab for them, half a dozen blueprints and both quarters rolled into traffic faster than he'd been able to a few minutes earlier.

The merciless Arizona sun beat down on him as he dodged cars to retrieve his now battered blueprints. Clutching the documents, Patrick felt as triumphant as he did every time he had made a touchdown in college. He returned to the parking meter. The single quarter he'd been able to recover bought him fifteen minutes, barely enough time to make the half-mile trek to the Goldwater Centre.

The intense heat began to take its toll. "Oh, but it's a dry heat," he said wryly to no one in particular, mimicking the words of the airline worker who'd only an hour and a half earlier informed him his luggage was en route to San Diego. Or maybe San Francisco.

By block two, Patrick had taken off his maroon silk tie, draping the costly accessory carelessly over his arm.

He had no idea why Winifred Longmont, the owner of this project, had insisted on this particular construction management firm. Tightening his grip on the blueprints, he was only sorry it wasn't the neck of the guy who'd made the red pen comments all over them. The generous use of red ink made his plans look as though they were practically bleeding.

With the pavement shimmering in the inferno and a slow, dry wind beginning to blow, the alien world seemed even hotter, and he felt as though he were in an oven. His mouth seemed as though it were stuffed with cotton, and he sensed his dried lips cracking. Perspiration plastered his hair to his head and trickle after trickle of sweat slid down his neck. If only he'd brought his motorcycle, he'd be at the Goldwater Centre by now, without the dripping. He'd figured out the advantages of a compact vehicle years ago.

He raised his head and wiped the dampness with an angry swipe of his hand. The skyline of Phoenix looked like a mix of bad 1960's and 70's architectural design to him. No way would he let somebody from this cowboy town tell him how to design an award-winning house. No way was he going to lose the Mitchell Burrell Medallion of Excellence this year. His firm needed both the recognition and the new business it would attract.

By block four, he'd rolled up his sleeves and undone the top two buttons of his damp, cream-colored linen shirt. He'd run out of things to take off without being arrested. He began to walk faster. Drenched with sweat, he didn't break stride as he burst through the double glass doors leading to the office building.

The Goldwater Centre appeared to be in the middle of a major renovation project. Dodging the drop-cloths and spattered paint buckets strewn about the expansive, two-story lobby, he nearly ran into the metal extension ladder propped against the wall. The heady scent of dust mixed with wet paint made him sneeze. He looked around for a building directory, seeing nothing but blank walls covered with fresh patches of dry wall spackle.

He jogged the entire length and breadth of the ground floor, only to discover that an employment agency and an insurance office were the sole tenants of the first story. Frustrated in his search, he headed for the elevator, punched the button, and impatiently paced the floor.

A worker in dusty overalls tapped him on the back. "It's out of order, pal. Stairs are over that way."

Nodding his thanks, Patrick bolted up the stairs to the second floor. The air in the stairwell, stale, oppressive, and, if possible, even hotter than the weather outside, seemed to close in on him. He struggled up several flights of stairs, scanning floor after floor of offices until he found himself on the twelfth floor.

A handwritten sign marked the temporary entrance to the J. S. Construction Management Firm. Patrick shoved open the door, knocking the make-shift identifier to the floor.

The receptionist looked like a high school girl. He should have known. His drawings sure looked as though someone had scribbled on them with a red crayon. Picturing her sitting in front of a television set doodling all over his precious blueprints, he grimaced. "I'd like to see the man in charge. Please."

As the sweat poured into his eyes faster than he could blink it out, he reached for his handkerchief. "Damn. No jacket. No handkerchief." He mopped his dripping forehead with his silk tie. "Good thing this is only my second favorite."

The girl at the desk handed him a box of Kleenex. "Hot enough for you?"

"It was hot enough for me about forty degrees ago."

"The boss will be back in a half hour or so. You look thirsty. Can I get you something to drink?"

"Thanks. That would be wonderful," he replied, wiping both sides of his neck. He might as well save his anger and frustration for the person who deserved it.

The young woman reappeared seconds later with a bottle of water and several women in tow.

"Thank you." Keeping an eye on the flock of females, he chugged the water and lobbed the empty bottle into a wastebasket on the other side of the room.

"Slam dunk," one of the women said as the others applauded. "The Suns could sure use you."

"Hey, I could use him," a plump redhead commented as she walked into the office lobby with another woman.

Jacki came to a sudden stop in the twelfth floor hallway. She couldn't believe what she saw. A row of women stood with their noses pressed against the glass doors and windows of her office suite. Inching her way past them, she slipped through the doorway.

The office lobby overflowed with women of all ages, shapes, and sizes, and they appeared to be throwing wads of paper at a wastebasket. A handsome man with a near perfect physique stood in the center of the room, surrounded by what seemed to be every female on the twelfth floor. And he wore one of the biggest grins she'd ever seen.

"Is there a problem here, Mia?" Jacki asked over the noise of the crowd. The guy was undeniably good-looking, but these women acted as though he were some kind of movie star or something.

"He wants to see the man in charge." Mia started giggling. The other women joined in, and soon the office rang with the sound of feminine laughter.

"They do this every time I ask to see the man in charge," the stranger chuckled.

Jacki wasn't amused. She held out her hand in a cold introduction. "I'm Jacqueline Santiago, and I'm the man in charge."

TWO

"Jacqueline, as in J. M. Santiago? You most definitely aren't a man." Patrick's look was fixed on her, but it wasn't on her face. "I apologize for my mistake."

She crossed her arms over her chest. Despite the fact his open appreciation annoyed her, Jacki blushed at his appraisal.

"Why don't we talk in my office?"

A chorus of "ooohs" followed them as they walked away from the crowd.

Jacki balled her fists and clenched her teeth while they went down the hallway. What was it with this guy? Who did he think he was, disrupting the office like that? He thought a man ran her business? It was all she could do to maintain her composure.

Once in her office, she motioned him to an oak chair near a small, matching table by the window. "Have a seat."

As he turned to sit, she noticed that perspiration soaked the back of his shirt. This heat was hard on everyone, and she certainly didn't intend to let him die right there in her office.

"I'm sorry about the air-conditioning." Trying to

muster up a businesslike smile, she only succeeded in producing a tight, thin line across her face. "We're doing some remodeling. Let me turn on this fan. It might help a little." She reached down and switched on the machine. The whirring sound of the blades filled the room.

"Would you like some water?" When it got there, she could decide whether to throw it on him or drown him in it.

"Thanks. Mia was nice enough to get me some, but I could sure use some more. Phoenix is a lot warmer than Portland."

"Portland, Oregon?"

"No, other side of the country. Portland, Maine."

She spoke into the intercom. "Mia, would you mind bringing us a pitcher of ice water?"

Mia appeared at her door almost instantly, two icy bottles of sparkling water in hand. "They're remodeling the kitchen now. We don't have running water, but there's a case of these in the fridge."

So much for drowning him, Jacki thought, watching as he and Mia exchanged amused looks. Sure, they could smile. They didn't have to worry about all the time this man had caused her office—and several others—to waste.

"Drink it all," Mia advised on her way out of the room.

Sitting down across from him, Jacki took a deep breath. "Is there something I can help you with?"

"Yes, there is." He stared at her intently.

Beginning to feel flustered by his unblinking gaze, she unrolled the blueprints, immediately recognizing her own red pen comments. "This is the Longmont project." In her opinion, the project from hell. She had never worked with or seen an architectural design so at odds with the desert environment and so full of potential building code violations as this one.

"You must be Mr. Godwin, Ms. Longmont's architect."

"Patrick." The smile he gave her would have dazzled a lesser female.

"Mr. Godwin." She tried to look him directly in the eye but couldn't seem to get past those full, sensual lips. "There's no way we're going to get building permits with these plans."

"What do you mean 'no way'?" He leaned forward. "These plans are perfectly acceptable in Maine." As his smile disappeared, the glint in his eyes took on a decidedly dangerous edge.

"But not in Phoenix." She returned the look with her own best razor sharp glare.

"I understand that you have different codes here in Arizona . . ."

"And a different climate," she interrupted. "And different zoning ordinances. And different architectural styles. And different tastes, none of which seems to have been taken into consideration." Let him chew on that for a while, she thought.

He didn't chew very long. "The agreement the owner has with you states that you would take care of the compliance with local codes and ordinances."

"That's what most of my comments deal with." She gestured to the blueprint with her pen.

"Those aren't the ones I have an issue with. We can talk about the specific local requirements. I can work with those. But I don't like the comments where

you question my design, my artistic ability. After all,
that's what I was hired to do—I *am* the architect."

"And I was hired to see to it that your design
works, comes in on budget, comes in on time, and
is buildable. After all, that's what I was hired to
do—I *am* the construction manager." The sound of
the ballpoint pen clicking punctuated her declara-
tion. She pointed with the tip. "Just look at these
plans. They're a mess."

"I suppose *you* could do a better design."

"Mr. Godwin, Mia could do a better design than
this. Heck, my dog Bart could do a better design if
he dipped his tail in ink and wagged it on a drawing
pad."

Patrick counted to twenty-five. "Then I take it Bart
helped out with your red-line comments." Jacqueline
Santiago was great looking, but he certainly didn't
intend to let her interference affect his chances at
the Mitchell Burrell Medallion of Excellence. He
needed it too badly to let anyone or anything get in
the way. Maybe if he could just soften her up a bit . . .

Ignoring Jacki's glare, he continued, "Listen, Ms.
Santiago, I only designed what Ms. Longmont truly
wants. Imagine, if you will, a piece of Maine right
here in the middle of the Arizona desert."

"She actually said that?" Jacki hooted as she stood.

"She sure did." He wrinkled his brow in annoy-
ance.

"Well, Ms. Longmont indicated to *me* that she was
looking for something entirely different. Imagine, if
you can," she flung her arms wide, "a Spanish haci-
enda in total harmony with the Arizona desert."

His look changed from irritation to disbelief. "She said that?"

"She most certainly did." Jacki put her hands on her hips.

"Then we have a problem . . . a damned big problem. I need to talk to Ms. Longmont as soon as I can. After all, she *is* the owner."

"Why don't we set up a meeting for tomorrow? We can meet back here in the morning, say at ten, and give her a call. Together."

Standing, Patrick offered her his hand. "I'll see you at ten."

A piece of Maine in the desert, my foot, Jacki thought, returning his handshake with a crushing grip.

She let out a long breath as she watched him leave her office. Good thing she'd sworn off men, because this one was a prime specimen. His thick, dark brown hair fell in waves to just past his collar. Lord, even his arms were sexy. Muscular forearms dusted with just the right amount of hair.

And those eyes. Blue as the heavens. Her cousin had discovered that particular phrase in one of those romances she was always reading, and it certainly fit Patrick Godwin.

The architect was the sexiest man she'd ever seen. For the first time in a long time, she wondered what a man's lips would feel like against hers. Feeling herself blush, she shook her head to jar her brain back to reality. Too bad his personality ruined the package.

"Some hunk," Mia noted, as if she'd read her mind.

"Really, Mia, how can you say that about Mr. Godwin?" Jacki's response sounded a little too abrupt even to her own ears. "He was all sweaty. He dripped all over my office. And that attitude . . ."

"He reminds me of Erik. You know, that guy who saves Selina."

"Selina who?" Jacki asked absently, bending down to pick up the mangled blueprints Patrick had left on her table.

"The beautiful Princess Selina from my new favorite romance, *Kiss Me a Thousand Times.*"

"You shouldn't read those books, Mia."

"You didn't seem to mind when I read you the good parts. You even had me repeat . . ."

"This is real life, Mia. I guarantee you that Mr. Godwin is no prince. We're not princesses. And you can only find romance in books."

At that very moment, Ms. Winifred Longmont was busy checking through her backpack, making sure she had her spare camera and enough film and batteries for the next six months. By now, Jacki and Patrick should be totally confused and not know what direction to take on her Arizona project. She smiled. Those two were perfect for each other. Patrick needed to settle down and Jacki needed to loosen up again. They'd be great together—they just didn't know it yet. She'd been very careful to give them conflicting instructions. That should give them something to talk about. And in the meantime . . . well, in the meantime, she intended to be having a grand adventure in Africa, capturing all of that wonderful wildlife on film and visiting the Sphinx.

* * *

Some man in charge, Patrick thought as he took the stairs down to the street level. He pictured Jacqueline Santiago all the way to his parking place. Mesmerizing green eyes. Hair that looked soft as black velvet.

And what a shape! And what a temper. Of course, he could have lived without that comment about her dog being a better designer than he was. He could tell she'd made the remark because she was barely able to contain her anger. Good thing he'd managed to stay so calm.

Later, at the hotel, Patrick felt no surprise when he found out that they'd lost his reservation.

The clerk in the charcoal gray power suit seemed vaguely insulted when he pointed this out to her. "Fortunately, we have more rooms available than usual," she explained while consulting her terminal. "After all, this is the off season."

"I can only begin to imagine the on season," Patrick observed with a sigh, adding his name to the blank room bill.

The clerk registered no emotion when Patrick told her the airline had lost his luggage. Not even a little pity. Likewise, she expressed no surprise when he told her he had no idea how long—or short—his stay would be. The clerk gave Patrick a well-practiced, impersonal smile, handed him the plastic key card, and wished him a happy stay.

Exhausted and rumpled, he trudged stiffly across the polished marble floor to the bank of elevators. It seemed forever before the next elevator appeared.

He pressed the button to the seventeenth floor. The droning elevator music almost put him to sleep before he reached his destination. He was mildly astonished the elevator worked properly and that it stopped at the right floor. He found his room with no problem, but it took him several attempts to get the key card to open the art deco door.

Taking no notice of the room itself, he stumbled to the bed, collapsing face first into the welcoming softness of the comforter. He fell asleep almost immediately, and when he began to dream, it was of a tall, raven-haired beauty with big, emerald eyes.

It was early morning when Patrick finally woke up, confused and disoriented. The morning sun was never this bright in Portland. Yawning loudly, he rubbed his hands over his stubbled face and remembered it all. The flight. His lost luggage. The heat. Goldwater Centre. The man in charge. Especially the man in charge.

He realized he was very, very hungry. When was the last time he'd eaten? Yesterday? Picking up the phone, he dialed room service, and ordered enough food for several people.

He headed toward the tiled bathroom for a long shower, leaving a trail of his once impeccable clothing. The rhythmic spray hammering from the dual shower heads was the best thing he'd felt in days. As he dried himself with the luxuriously thick towel, he eyed his dirty clothes through the open bathroom door with distaste. Normally, he thought, he would have sent them out to be cleaned. No, normally, he corrected himself, he would have had a suitcase full of nice, clean clothes. He removed the shirt and slacks from the floor and shook them as hard as he could. It didn't help. He shrugged into his clothing, wrinkling his nose in disgust at the stains, odors, and creases.

Room service came just as he finished dressing. Starving, he ate the crisp bacon even before the waiter left the room.

After making short work of breakfast, he put his tie in the cleaner's bag provided by the hotel. Maybe they could save it. Suddenly, he remembered his suitcase. Another lengthy call to the airline provided him with the information that they'd located his luggage, and it should be there within the next twenty-four hours.

Glancing up at the mirror above the phone, he couldn't ever remember looking this disheveled, especially after a shower. And he had forgotten to shave. He rubbed his two-day old beard, returned to the bathroom, and rummaged though the courtesy kit provided by the hotel. The pink plastic disposable razor and the bar of deodorant soap spelled disaster. Patrick ended up with more nicks and cuts on his face than he had the first time he shaved at age thirteen. Tearing off small pieces of tissue, he stuck one on each wound. It would have to do.

He looked in the mirror again. A face covered with red badges of courage stared back. The body belonged to a stranger. Godwins never looked this hideous. Then he grinned—Winnie Longmont would probably see this as an improvement. She'd always considered the Godwins to be overly stuffy.

Patrick decided no matter how urgently he needed

to see Ms. Santiago, he would buy a new set of clothes. Clean clothes.

Gulping the last of his freshly squeezed orange juice, he grabbed his key card and headed toward the elevator.

The only clothing store open this early was two doors down from the hotel and specialized in costume Western wear. Patrick looked at the bright embroidery, pearlized buttons, sparkling fringe, and colorful yokes on the shirts hanging on the racks in the front of the store. "I'd have to be drunk or dead to wear this," he said to himself.

He noticed some plain blue workshirts near the rear of the store. The first one he found fit. Jeans and a plain brown leather belt completed his first Arizona ensemble.

He walked over to the store's full-length mirror. The jeans were adequate. The shirt fit. But his face . . . oh, no. Sheepishly, he removed a dozen blood-soaked pieces of blue tissue and stuffed them into his pocket.

Turning, he looked at himself from behind. The jeans were snug. So snug, they felt like a second skin. Maybe he should buy the next size up.

A shapely brunette in a Western shirt studded with rhinestones was trying on cowboy hats at a nearby table. She glanced his way. "Very nice," she commented, winking at him. "Very, very nice."

He decided to keep the jeans. Giving the woman a killer smile, he grabbed a package of underwear from a nearby stand and walked up to the front of the store to pay for his selections. He heard a feminine attempt at a wolf whistle behind him as he made his way to the cashier. Maybe staying here a while wasn't going to be so bad after all.

THREE

The elevator at the Goldwater Centre still wasn't working, so Patrick took his time on the long climb up the stairs to the J. S. Construction Management Firm.

Mia was the first to spot him. She stopped snapping her bubblegum. "Look who's here!" she said with obvious delight.

"Mia! Great to see you again. You been practicing that hook shot?"

"Just you watch." She crumpled up the nearest piece of paper, took aim, and sunk the shot.

"Great throw. That practice paid off." He winked at her. "Is your boss around?"

"Jacki! Come here!" Mia called, ignoring all the expensive communications technology on her desk that would have allowed her to page her cousin in a much quieter way.

"Mia, how many times do I have to tell you . . . Mr. Godwin! What a surprise. You're early."

Her gaze drawn to his lips, she forgot what she was going to say next. Patrick exuded maleness. In fact, he filled the room with it.

His chestnut hair seemed wavier, more casual today. A lock of that beautiful hair fell forward on his forehead, and she stifled the urge to reach up and push it back into place.

Jacki had been around construction sites on an almost daily basis since she was a kid, but darned if she could remember a plain blue workshirt looking this good on anyone. There ought to be a law. Now, what was she saying?

"We didn't expect you here until ten. You're very early."

For all Patrick knew, Jacki might have been reciting "Ode to a Grecian Urn." He was totally overcome by her presence. She was tall. Only a couple of inches shorter than he was. He didn't know many women that tall. In fact, right now, for the life of him, he couldn't summon up the image of any other woman. Her magnificent, sable-colored hair was pulled back in a single braid and secured with a simple leather thong. Yet a few stubborn wispy curls had already worked their way out of their confinement. Her golden brown skin was clear and smooth, free of cosmetics. A sprinkling of freckles across the bridge of her nose prevented her classical beauty from being too severe. Patrick visualized his lips following that trail of freckles, kiss by kiss by kiss.

Patrick's gaze traveled down her long, lovely neck. Her malachite pendant, shaped like an arrowhead, pointed directly to the suggestive swell of her breasts, which, to his way of thinking, were overly camouflaged by her silk shirt.

And her eyes. He hadn't been imagining their gorgeous green. Had there ever been a lovelier woman? Jacki Santiago was no desert mirage. This was the real thing. It was going to be a pleasure being in the same room with her again, even if they'd be at each other's throats the whole time.

Mia tapped her on the shoulder. "Jacki, the conference room is available." She gestured to a room off the lobby. "I'll bring in some coffee and you guys can make that phone call."

"Oh, the phone call. Right." Jacki ushered Patrick to a small room. A telephone sat in the center of a table. As he sat down directly in front of the phone and began to pull it toward him, she shot over to the place across from him, leaned over the table, and picked up the receiver. Triumphantly, she pulled a piece of paper from her pocket and began to punch in Winifred Longmont's office phone number. He punched in the final digit, brushing her fingers in the process.

She didn't understand it. She wanted to crush his fingers under the handset. Why was she having such a hard time moving her hand away from his?

Patrick thought that he could sit like this all day, maybe all week. The view was beautiful. The view was bountiful. And the view smelled heavenly. He sighed happily.

"Coffee, anyone?" At the sound of Mia's voice, Jacki jerked her hand away and stepped back, phone in hand.

Taking the handset from Jacki, Patrick spoke into it, "Yes, we're here. Sorry about that. We were just having a little . . . mechanical difficulty. You know how that is . . ."

Jacki glared at him. He smiled and took the cup

from Mia. Nodding when she held up the carton of creamer, he moved the cup toward her.

Mia showed him the dish of sugar packets. He held up two fingers.

"Yes, this is Patrick Godwin. Is this Carole? How did you know it was me?" He paused, settling back into his chair. Accepting a spoon from Mia, he began to stir his coffee. "I think you have a very nice voice, too."

"I think you have a nice voice, Patrick," Mia echoed in the background.

"Mia, I hear the phone ringing," whispered Jacki.

Mia shook her head. "I don't."

Narrowing her eyes, Jacki pointed toward the door. "Yes, you do."

At the sound of a phone ringing in another office, Mia backed out of the room. "Gee, cuz, you must be psychic."

Patrick continued to stir his coffee.

Why didn't the man drink it black like normal people? The clinking of the spoon against the ceramic cup was driving her crazy. She felt like wrenching it out of his hand and whacking him with it.

"This is a speaker phone, Mr. Godwin." Irritated, Jacki pushed the speaker button, and Carole's sugary voice filled the air. "Good morning, Ms. Browne," Jacki sat down, her own voice coming out more saccharine than sugar.

"Are you with someone, Patrick?"

Carole apparently didn't recognize *her* voice, Jacki thought. What was it about this guy that made women turn to half-set Jell-O? Just hearing him made them act like teenagers.

"I'm here in Phoenix with Jacqueline Santiago, your construction manager." He tapped his spoon on the edge of his cup and laid it on his napkin.

"Oh. Hello, Jacki."

Jacki smiled at the sudden frost in Carole's voice. Not one bit sorry that she had spoiled their flirtatious exchange, and relieved that Patrick had finally stopped stirring a hole in his cup, she got right to the point. "May we please speak to Ms. Longmont?"

There was a long pause from the other end of the phone. "Winnie? You want to talk to Winnie? Just a second."

After a loud click, Winifred Longmont's voice came over the machine.

"Hello, Jacki and hello, Patrick."

Both of them began to return her greeting, but Winnie's voice continued on.

"I hope that Carole didn't let the cat out of the bag. I know how she'll tell you almost anything, Patrick. Isn't it amazing, Jacki, how he can charm the socks off any female within a hundred mile radius? I'll bet there are a lot of barefoot women in Phoenix just about now." Winnie chuckled at her own corny joke.

Patrick's smile began to look uncertain. Jacki merely grunted.

"Well, kids, you may have figured out by now that this is a pre-recorded tape."

Patrick's smile disappeared. Jacki's mouth dropped open.

"I'm not in the country right now. In fact, I'm in Africa on a photography safari. Patrick, you remember—the one that you said I simply had to take before I was too old to enjoy it."

Jacki threw him an accusatory look. For once, he actually looked contrite.

"And Jacki, you were right. I need to see the Pyramids. Thanks for lending me those travel books on Africa. They really were so helpful. Carole will be sending them back to you shortly."

It was Patrick's turn to give her a look. Jacki flushed guiltily.

"So, I'll be off on my African adventure. From Egypt to the Cape of Good Hope—should take, oh, about six months . . ."

Both Jacki and Patrick leaped out of their chairs and leaned toward the phone.

"What? Gone for six months?" Patrick hit the table with the palm of his hand. "She can't do that!"

"Six months!" sputtered Jacki. "Why, the major part of the project will be finished by then!"

". . . and I'm counting on both of you to work together to complete my house." Winnie's taped voice continued. "I'm sure that between the two of you, things will work out just fine. After all, I have hired two of the most talented young people there are. Now, remember, I want it on time, on budget and published in that architectural magazine. You know. The one with all those big, beautiful pictures. 'Bye for now, kids. Talk to you again in six months."

The line went dead.

Patrick exhaled a long breath. "So much for getting direction from Winnie."

"Oh, she gave us direction, all right. It looks like

we're stuck with each other for the duration." Jacki shook her head at the thought.

"At least we know what each one of us is supposed to do. I design the building."

"And I make it work. When was the last time you saw a house in an architectural magazine that came in on time and on budget?"

"Never." He shrugged.

"I thought so. But this one will. Even if one or both of us die trying." She grabbed the plans from the corner of the room. "Let's get started."

The meeting dragged on for six solid hours following their call to Winnie, and it still wasn't going well. Yesterday Patrick had been too friendly. Today he was even more friendly. But not to her. The man oozed charm at everyone from the bakery lady to the window cleaners. She certainly didn't intend to fall victim to it. That is, if he should ever decide to direct it her way. Which he hadn't, so far. Watching the female office staff slobber all over him had been bad enough. Jacki wasn't about to fall at his feet like the rest of the women in the office. Although she had to admit that he did clean up pretty good.

She kept trying to get down to business. All he wanted to do was flirt with Mia and any other female who happened to be in the building—except her. And finally, she lost it.

"Would you please stop encouraging all of these women to come in here?" Jacki snapped. "I can't even get a full sentence finished before one of your admirers is poking her head through my door. Some of them, I've never seen before."

"That sounded pretty much like a couple of full sentences to me, and no one's come in."

She shot him a look that she hoped would express the full force of her anger and frustration.

"Really, I'm not doing anything to encourage them . . ." He gave her a gorgeous smile that started small and winning, and grew to radiant and totally captivating even as she watched.

"There." She pointed at his offending lips.

"What?"

"That's it. You're doing it again. But it's not working. This is me, not one of your instant groupies." Which was, judging by the rapid thumping of her heart, one of the biggest whoppers she'd told in her life.

"What's 'it'? I still don't know what you're talking about."

Picking up her pen, she began clicking it in agitation. "Wipe that movie star grin off your face, and I'll tell you."

"Movie star grin?" His smile broadened even more as he laid his hand on her arm. "You think I have a movie star grin? Ruth, my secretary back home, calls it my used car salesman smile."

She brushed away the trespassing hand with her pen. "Smart woman."

Chuckling at her reaction, he agreed. "She should be. She had thirty years of experience before I hired her."

"What kind of experience? With car salesmen?"

"No. Keeping 'impudent young architects' in line, as she puts it."

"She sure has you pegged."

"I'd love to continue this discussion," Patrick interrupted as he stood. "We could even cover my shallow personality," he murmured, bending so close to her their lips almost touched. "But I have better things to do."

"Better things?" She could feel her traitorous lips begin to pucker up.

Reaching for her hand, he gave it a firm, businesslike shake. "Have a nice day, Ms. Santiago."

As she felt her blood drain from her face to her ankles, it was all she could do to keep from stabbing him through the heart with her pen. "You—you—architect!" she screeched after him.

As she watched him go, she adjusted her cuffs and her attitude.

"Holy moley, Jacki," Mia whispered to her, "what are you trying to do? Lose a megabucks account?"

"Sometimes, Mia, I wish you would use real swear words. We're all grown-ups here, you know." Jacki jammed a fistful of papers into her briefcase.

"You're the one who made me clean up my language," Mia reminded her. "You said it wasn't professional to swear. But I'll tell you what's not professional: the way you treated Patrick today. In fact, I've never seen you treat anyone like that. Not even old Fish Face after he broke off your engagement."

Jacki walked rapidly toward the staircase with Mia trying to catch up to her. Her cousin closed the gap on the ground floor.

"Evan. His name is Evan. And the way I treat Mr.

Godwin is my business. I really don't know if I can work with that heap of hormones at all," Jacki finally responded as the automatic doors opened before them. "He's the most insufferable, superficial, un-focused—"

"Hunk." Mia finished the sentence with a sigh.

"Frankly, I don't care if he's Antonio Banderas. The man is an ass," Jacki declared emphatically as they walked across the shimmering hot pavement and climbed into her Cherokee.

FOUR

He was stirring his damn coffee again. As Jacki walked toward her office the next morning, she heard Patrick before she saw him.

Making an abrupt turn, she headed straight for Mia's desk. "Mia, this is going to be a difficult project as it is. But if you really want to make some points with me, don't ever serve Mr. Godwin's coffee in a ceramic cup again. Give the man a styrofoam one. That infernal clinking is driving me crazy."

"What do you mean?"

Putting her head down by Mia's, she whispered, "Listen. Just listen." To Jacki it sounded like the bells of Notre Dame.

"You mean that little tapping noise? I can barely hear it."

"Little? Maybe that's what stir-crazy really means. Make a note to buy styrofoam cups. Big ones, so he doesn't have to refill them."

"But cuz, you said they were bad for the environment."

"Then buy the kind that can be recycled. There's such a thing as noise pollution." Wincing as she left, Jacki called over her shoulder. "Oh, and Mia?"

"Yes?"

"Get a box of those plastic stirrers, too. We're going to soundproof an architect."

By the time Jacki got to her office, Patrick had finished dissolving the sugar in his coffee, and apparently made himself at home. He'd moved everything off her table, spread his own stuff all over the room, and was in the process of changing the station on her radio. The high-pitched twanging of an electric guitar surrounded her. She cringed. "Lose my station, and you're dead meat."

He spun around at the sound of her voice. "Good morning! Just trying to find some mood music." He began to play an air guitar in time to the beat.

Was this some kind of weird, universal guy thing or what? Jacki thought, thoroughly annoyed. Were all men born with an air guitar strapped to their hip?

As though reading her mind, he stopped his one-man imaginary concert. "Want some coffee? Mia left a whole pot of it and some extra cups."

She was doomed. How was she going to stand weeks of listening to this alternative rock crap accompanied by the percussion of a clinking teaspoon? She stomped over to the drafting table.

"And what is this?"

"Just tightening up some details. Take a look. I borrowed your building code book."

"Tightening up some details? It looks like you're trying to figure out how to attach the shutters when we haven't even decided whether or not there will be any shutters at all." She raised her voice over the music.

Patrick walked over to the stereo and turned down

the volume. "You don't have to yell. I can hear you okay." He picked up his coffee cup and took a sip. Frowning, he reached for the spoon again and stuck it back in the cup.

"We talked about this yesterday. You agreed to make some revisions." She flipped through the drawings on her table. "The shutters are still in. All of them. And the clapboard siding. The dormers. The widow's walk. Where are the revisions? What in the world do you think you're building? Some lighthouse or something?"

"The style is Cape Cod. Winnie wanted Maine, and I'm giving her Maine."

"Then give her Maine in New England. There is no way I'm building a Cape Cod house in the middle of the Arizona desert." The crescendo of her voice and the sound of his stirring reached a feverish pitch.

"Actually, this is a modernistic interpretation of a Cape Cod. It's not a true Cape Cod. No one has ever created an interpretation like this before. It's a shoo-in for the Mitchell Burrell Medallion of Excellence."

Three hours into their meeting, Jacki began to wonder if they'd ever agree on anything even mildly related to the Longmont project. He still thought he would win his precious architectural award with his "innovative" modernistic Cape Cod style.

Jacki decided it was up to her to break their impasse. "Since we don't agree on the style at this point, let's just talk about the schedule."

"All right. Winnie wants this house done by Thanksgiving." Patrick started making notes.

Taking the calendar from the wall and laying it in front of them, Jacki flipped through the pages.

"Counting this month, that gives us about six months to redesign, get permits, and build it."

He raised his eyebrow. "It's going to be tight."

"Well, at least we agree on something." She turned the calendar back to July.

"How long does it take to build a custom home like this out here?"

She clicked her pen as she thought. "I'm going to need at least five months on my end because of the summer rains. She looked down at the calendar. "That means I can only give you two weeks for the redesign. We have to get the foundation poured before the monsoons begin."

She glanced at her watch. "I'm sorry, Mr. Godwin, I'm afraid I have another appointment now." It figured. They finally had something they agreed on.

"More important than me?"

"Maybe not more important, but a heck of a lot easier," she sighed.

"Easier is never better," he advised her, picking up his notes and leaving the room.

Itching to get back to work on the Longmont project, Jacki rushed through her next appointment. She had just sat down at her drafting table when Mia materialized in her doorway.

"So, how was your meeting with Patrick? He's one hunkalicious kind of guy."

"Hunkalicious? I really hadn't noticed." Jacki adjusted the paper in front of her.

Mia peered intently at Jacki's face. "Your nose is growing."

"It is not." Jacki jerked open her drawer and took out a mechanical pencil. "He's nothing to write home about."

"Right. You need to get your head examined or your eyes checked. One or the other. Maybe both. That man is something to send a gold-plated telegram by way of a rocketship home about."

"He might be mildly easy on the eyes, but I can't see why women attach themselves to him like . . . the lint on these slacks." She plucked a tiny thread from a spot near her knee.

Mia leaned her elbows on the table. "Forget about your clothes. What did you talk about while you were in there with him? What did you find out about him?"

"Nothing exciting. What's there to find out?"

"I'd want to know all the important stuff." Mia bent forward. "Like, is he married?"

"The subject never came up. If he is, I pity his poor wife having to compete with the mindless hordes."

Impatiently, her cousin interrupted. "Tell me what you know. Everything. Or I won't give you a moment's peace until you do, *prima.*"

Jacki sighed. "Honest, we didn't talk about his personal life at all. For all I know, he has three wives and fourteen children. And I don't care whether he does or not."

"You *really* didn't find out anything about him?"

"That's right. I told you we didn't discuss anything personal, period."

"If I was with Patrick Godwin, there'd be no talking at all." Mia straightened up, leaving the office before Jacki could close her mouth.

After staring at the empty spot her cousin had occupied, Jacki realized she'd been daydreaming not about the project, but about Patrick. About the way that one lock of hair fell on his forehead. About the slight strain of the denim shirt across his broad shoulders. About the curl of those kissable lips when he smiled at other women.

Thinking about him was a waste of her time. And speaking of time, she didn't think she had any other meetings scheduled for that afternoon. Just to be sure, she walked over to her computer to check her electronic calendar.

The stacks of paperwork on the desk were forgotten as she stared at the computer screen. Ignoring the very communications technology she kept reminding her cousin to use, she yelled, "Mia Alvarez! Where are you? Get in here this minute!"

"So, what do you think of your new screen saver?" Mia giggled after responding to Jacki's order.

"Where's my other screensaver? Where are my fish?" Jacki's eyes were riveted to the screen. "What have you done with my fish?"

"Fish are boring. You needed something . . . sexier."

"An animated screen saver with a man removing his clothing has no place in this office." Jacki sank slowly into her chair, her gaze never leaving the cyberstripper.

"I don't know what's wrong with you. Your fish had no clothes at all. They were naked. A man's an animal, just like a fish. Only without scales. What's the big deal?" Mia pushed Jacki's head, now center screen, to one side and leaned over her shoulder.

Together, they stared at the computer. The animated male was down to his last article of clothing. Grinning broadly, he took it off.

Jacki shook her head in disbelief, regretting, not for the first time, her promise to her late uncle that Mia would always have a place in the family business.

"That looks like a big deal to me." Mia began to giggle again.

"Get this off my screen. Now. Before someone else sees it. I don't want them to think I'm . . ."

"Human? A woman?"

"You don't have to think about sex all the time to be a real woman."

"Not if you're dead."

"Watch it, *prima,*" Jacki warned, turning around in her seat to look at her cousin. "If you're not careful—"

"And if you're not careful, you'll end up just like Sister Agnes. You used to be a lot more fun." Mia flounced out, leaving Jacki alone with her computer.

There was no dealing with Mia when she was in this kind of mood. Jacki looked at the screen. Where did Mia get this stuff anyway? Mr. Cyberstripper was starting his show all over again. She didn't have time to figure out how to evict him from her computer, but Mia would know.

Sighing with deep resignation, Jacki closed the door to her office, knowing that if she did so, no one would bother her.

Walking over to her bookcase, she took out several volumes on architectural design. Hours passed before she returned to her computer. She jiggled the mouse a couple of times to make her unwanted cyberguest, who was still at it, disappear.

The phone rang, but she ignored it. Eventually, the caller wisely gave up, and there was a welcome silence. After an hour or so, the phone rang again. Startled out of her research, Jacki picked up the receiver.

"Yes?"

A feminine voice responded, "I knew you'd still be at the office. Isn't it past time for you to come home? I left hours ago."

Jacki looked out her office window at the lights below twinkling in the darkness. "Oh, hi, Mia! I was doing a little research, and time got away from me."

"Since when did you become a librarian? We've got a great staff, so delegate. You work too hard. You've got no social life, so to speak. And I worry about you. Especially since your former fiancé, whatever his name was, dumped you."

Jacki felt her temper flare, then dim when she heard the concern in her cousin's voice. Reaching for the jar of marbles on the top of the desk, she took out a few and began arranging the smooth, cold spheres as she talked. "You're right. Sort of. Here, I'm turning off my computer now. Listen." Clicking on the shut down prompt, she held the receiver to the machine until the whirring noise stopped. "See. Mr. Cyberstripper's been put to bed—alone, I might add—and I'm ready to go home. I just feel like I need to keep a tight rein on this project so it comes out okay. And as you know, sometimes that means working late."

"But research? What's so special about the Longmont project? Except the gorgeous architect, that is."

Wishing that Mia didn't know her so well, Jacki

answered calmly, "This is something I need to look at before our meeting tomorrow morning."

As the marbles cascaded through her fingers and clattered into the jar, she gently placed the receiver in its cradle. Once again involved with her reading, she didn't notice when one of the building's cleaning crew came into her office. Jumping up when someone reached around her chair and grabbed the wastebasket, she put her hand on her wildly beating heart as though that would calm it.

"I'm so sorry, Ms. Santiago. I thought you heard me. I didn't mean to scare you to death."

"That's okay, Curtis."

The custodian took the wire wastebasket from her office and returned with the empty receptacle, setting it quietly beside her desk.

Jacki yawned, stretched her hands over her head, and leaned back in her chair. She sat motionless for a few minutes, thinking about the next day's meeting, confident the discussion would go well.

Slowly walking to the door, she glanced around the office one last time. Her eyes rested on a snapshot of Bart, grinning, on her desk. *Pobrecito* puppy, she thought sadly. He hadn't seen enough of her lately, she lamented. She could always tell when her dog missed her. Bart seemed to get into more trouble than usual when he was feeling neglected.

"Soon," Jacki said to the photo. "In just a few months, this project will be at a point where I can take some time off." With that thought, she straightened the Diego Rivera print on the wall, gave her plant one last spritz of water, flicked off the lights and walked down the hallway to the lobby. Curtis was there, busily vacuuming the floor. He looked up as she passed by.

"Good night, Curtis."

"Good night, ma'am." He gave her a mock salute. Smiling, Jacki returned the gesture.

On the way out, she stopped at Mia's desk to use the telephone, calling down to the security guard in the lobby to let him know she was on her way. She stepped outside of the office into the dimly lit hallway that led to the elevators and punched the down button. As she waited, she rotated her neck to ease some of the tension. When the newly repaired elevator doors finally slid open, two more cleaning people rolled their cart into the hallway. Entering the empty elevator, she leaned back against the padded wall and closed her eyes. When the doors opened, she was mildly disappointed. It would have been nice to relax just a bit more before beginning the long journey home.

The guard greeted her at the security station. "Ms. Santiago, another late night? You look beat."

She smiled weakly.

"If you don't mind my telling you, you put in way too many hours. It's just not healthy for a young woman like you to wear herself out like this. If you're too tired to drive, I could call a cab for you."

"No thanks, Ray, I'll be fine. Really."

The security guard shook his bald head as he escorted Jacki out of the building to her car.

FIVE

The next morning, Jacki steered her Cherokee with one hand as she turned on the cell phone. She listened as the phone dialed the number, and was surprised to hear Mia's cheery voice. "J. S. Construction Management!"

"What are you doing there so early, Mia? I didn't hear you leave the house. My gosh, it isn't even six-thirty."

"I was just finishing up my term paper. It's due in less than an hour and a half," Mia replied.

"Is this another one of those last minute things? When did you start it?"

"No, this isn't another one of 'those last minute things.' The hard drive on our home computer died a dreadful death this morning, and I knew you wouldn't mind if I finished the paper here at work. I didn't wait until the last minute this time. I started it last night."

Jacki chuckled. "Did you get those styrofoam cups yet?"

"A whole case of them."

"And the plastic stirrers?"

"A thousand of them."

"Great. Thanks. I guess that's all for now then. No. Wait. One more thing. Have you killed the naked guy on my computer screen yet?"

But her cousin, in an untypical burst of efficiency, had already hung up.

After all the research she'd accomplished the night before and all the useful information she'd found, Jacki felt great. In fact, she felt so good she started singing along with the oldies station on the radio. She chimed in enthusiastically when one of her favorite Beatles songs began to play. None of that alternative stuff Patrick listened to polluted the airwaves in her car.

Several tunes later, Jacki was in the Goldwater Centre, still humming, this time to the elevator music. She swung open the door to J. S. Construction Management, and gave Mia, who was banging away on the computer keyboard, a tuneful greeting.

"Good morning . . ."

Mia looked up long enough to grin. "Does this good mood have anything to do with your eight o'clock appointment?"

Nothing bothered Jacki this morning. "Could be."

Jacki boogied back to her office. Whirling around, she belted one last tuneful warning, "Don't be late for your claaaaaass . . ."

"Son of a biscuit, look at the time!" Mia snatched up a stack of papers from the tray of her laser printer and dashed out the door.

There was no one at the reception desk when Patrick arrived ten minutes early for their eight o'clock meeting. He stood there a moment, not knowing what to do, then followed the sound of someone singing to the large conference room.

Jacki was leaning over the table, studying something on a blueprint. Patrick decided this was one woman who looked good from all angles. He lingered in the doorway, admiring this particular view with open appreciation.

Jacki glanced at him over her shoulder. "Good morning, Mr. Godwin."

He'd been up most of the night sketching some ideas. But right now he'd very much like to sketch her—she made quite a picture. "Good morning. Where's the coffee?"

"Let's skip the coffee for a while and get right to work." She seemed eager to start.

He spotted the coffee in the corner behind her. "Won't take but a minute. I'm not worth anything without my caffeine fix."

She waited until he'd filled his cup, then pointed to the chair opposite hers. "Go ahead and sit down, Mr. Godwin."

"Patrick," he corrected, soundlessly dissolving his double dose of sugar with the plastic stir stick.

Jacki smiled, relishing the silence of his actions. One problem down. Nine million to go. "Mr. Godwin. I understand that the Mitchell Burrell award means a lot to both you and Winnie. But I think there's a way we can win it without using the Cape Cod concept."

He nodded slowly, still stirring. "I was thinking along those same lines myself. In fact, I've sketched out some Macedonian style facades." He reached for one of the books laid out on the table, flipped to the index, and pointed to an example.

"I was thinking that Egyptian might be a unique style for the Longmont Project. It originated in a desert climate, and it's certainly not overdone around here." She laid her book on top of his, opening it to the place she'd marked the night before. "Take this column, for instance. See the simple lines, the elegant base . . ."

Her comments gave him an idea. "Yes, it's a very nice column." Envisioning one like it in the front area of Winnie's house, a design began to take shape. He picked up both books, one still inside the other. "I'm sorry. I need to run. We'll have to continue this later. I'd like to stay, but I've got to get back to the hotel. I have some urgent business to take care of." Patrick really was sorry he couldn't stay and just spend the rest of the morning gazing at her loveliness, but he'd just had a flash of inspiration, and he needed to get it down on paper while it was still fresh in his mind.

Jacki couldn't hide the look of shock on her face. "But, but . . . What about the rest of the meeting? We still have to discuss—"

"I'll call you later," he said briskly. "We'll set up a meeting sometime in the next day or so. Mind if I take your book with me?" Without waiting for her to answer one way or the other, Patrick left the room with both texts.

He had some nerve. Jacki gritted her teeth. She'd worked most of the night on his project, and he didn't even have the decency to stick around for the details.

Prior to this, she'd never done such in-depth research for clients unless they'd specifically requested it. His stupid design and that dumb award. That was all that mattered to him. If it weren't for Winnie, Jacki would let his ship in the great desert—or whatever he was planning—go down with the rats. But Winnie Longmont was one of her dearest friends, and Jacki just couldn't do that to her.

Slowly, she stacked the remaining books and stood. Who was she kidding? The main purpose of her research had been to make Patrick see how wrong he was and how right she was. How could he see the error of his ways if he didn't even stay long enough to ask questions or pore over the texts with her? How could he praise her for her clever suggestions if he left without hearing them? Jacki sighed.

Mia stuck her head in the conference room. "Jacki, maybe if you leave now, you can still make that library construction meeting." She had Jacki's briefcase in her hand.

"Are you already back from class?"

"Yeah. Miss me? There was no final. I only had to hand in my paper. So are you going to the meeting or not?"

Jacki rolled her eyes.

"Don't look at me that way! Come on, this is one of your pet projects. Mrs. Hermann will have one of her famous pretend heart attacks if you don't show up."

The image brought a smile to Jacki's lips. She'd had to back out of the library construction meeting at the last moment because of her appointment with Patrick. Now that the time slot was available again, she could go. Mrs. Hermann, a regular client as well as the chairperson of the building committee for the new annex to the children's library, had volunteered Jacki's time and expertise for the project.

"Okay, Mia. Fortunately, I didn't wear jeans today," Jacki said, smoothing the wrinkles from her turquoise silk pantsuit.

"Yes, I noticed you were all dressed up today. For some reason."

"I always try to dress appropriately for client meetings!" Jacki gave Mia what she hoped was a wide-eyed, innocent look.

"Whatever you say," Mia said. "Just don't expect me to buy it," she added, tossing the briefcase to Jacki. "Want me to call Mrs. Hermann and let her know that you're on your way?"

"No, I think I'll just show up. The meeting's probably already started." Jacki swung her purse strap over her shoulder, and picked up her briefcase. "Oh, and by the way, if Patrick Godwin calls while I'm gone, please give him my cell phone number." She stopped at the door. "One more thing—the only screensaver I want to see on my computer when I get back is one filled with fins and scales."

Patrick sat in the vacant office in the far back corner of the J.S. Construction Management Firm. The room was used mostly for storage, but at least it had an old drafting table and a beat-up task light. If Jacki knew that Mia had issued him a key to her offices, she'd go ballistic.

He wished he had another place to work, but the

project schedule was so tight he hadn't had time to look for an office of his own. Mia told him he could use this room during his stay in Phoenix—as long as he didn't slip up and let Jacki know about it. He had to be careful not to get caught, because the beautiful Ms. Santiago was known to work long hours. Besides, there was no way he wanted to get Mia in trouble with her boss—even if they were cousins.

It was a good thing he'd left Jacki's morning meeting when he did or he'd have lost the inspiration. It had come to him while she discussed Egyptian architecture. Maybe he'd even mention her in his acceptance speech when he won the Mitchell Burrell Medallion of Excellence.

He really needed to win the medallion. Now that he'd left the firm he used to be with and opened his own office back in Portland, that prestigious award would bring in all sorts of new clients clamoring for his architectural expertise. And Winnie's project would be featured in every architectural journal from New York to Tokyo.

Everyone else had gone home by six, and he'd been working hard at this redesign for hours. He kept sketching, surrounded by a rapidly growing mountain of crumpled, rejected drawings. He welcomed the silence of the office. Working alone suited him. It always had. Stretching, he decided he needed a strong cup of coffee to keep going. According to his watch, it was already eleven o'clock, Phoenix time. Two o'clock in Portland. Well, he wasn't leaving until the conceptual design was perfect, even if it took the rest of the night to do it.

Poking his head out of the door, he looked both

ways down the hall. The coast was clear. Jacki must have
finally gone home. He headed toward the coffeemaker.
The hallway was eerie—no illumination except for
the occasional security light. He tried to flick on the
fluorescent lights in the kitchen, but they weren't
hooked up yet, so he began digging through the cabi-
nets in the dark, trying to find the coffee by feel.

"We're going to get Winnie's house finished before they get these lights hooked up," he muttered
to himself.

As the fragrant brew began to drip through the machine, he searched for a real mug, but came up empty-
handed. Forced to use one of the styrofoam cups
stacked on the counter, he shuddered. Just the feel of
that synthetic material made his skin crawl. Besides,
why would someone as intelligent and enlightened as
Jacki Santiago stockpile something so detrimental to
the environment? Perhaps she didn't realize how bad
they were. He'd point that out to her tomorrow morning.

SIX

Patrick was going to hear the rest of her ideas and suggestions today whether he wanted to or not. Even if she had to tie him down to get him to listen to all the research she'd worked so hard to put together.

Jacki waited quietly for him in her office like a cat waiting for an unsuspecting lizard to stop long enough for it to pounce. Standing by her office window, she watched as he sauntered up the walkway. She might be twelve stories up, but she'd know him and his confident walk anywhere. He seemed to be in a good mood. That meant his charm would be at a particularly lethal level. No matter, she was strong enough to withstand close proximity to an irresistible, handsome man and feel nothing. Especially where this irresistible, handsome man was concerned.

Walking to her desk, she picked up the stack of architectural books that had been sitting there for two days now. After checking the titles, she pushed the speaker phone button. "Mia, I'm expecting Mr. Godwin momentarily. Let me know when he gets here."

"You already told me that once this morning. Is

he coming here twice? Or are you just anxious? I can't wait to see him, either. That man sure is a hunk."

Jacki sighed. "Please don't refer to our clients as 'hunks'."

"Most of them aren't, so you don't have to worry about that," Mia laughed.

"I only worry about you running our front desk in a professional manner."

"Oh, quit being such a worrywart for a minute and just admit he's the best looking client we've ever had. In fact, he's the biggest studmuffin ever to set foot in our office."

"Stop it, Mia! I don't want Mr. Godwin hearing from your lips that he's a studmuffin."

"Don't worry. He just heard it from you."

Male laughter followed the unwelcome revelation. Jacki sank into the cushions of her desk chair, wondering if it were possible to drop dead from sheer mortification. She knew her blood pressure had to be at stroke level.

Mia popped into Jacki's office. "Mr. Godwin's here."

"Thanks for the advance warning," Jacki hissed. "Can't you just tell him I'm not in?"

"Not in? Now why would she want to tell me something like that?" Patrick asked as he entered the office.

She prayed for a bolt of lightning. Anything to put her out of her misery fast. Her silent pleas ignored, she'd just have to lie her way out of this. She could lie. Even her priest would understand this situation.

Averting her eyes, she turned on the computer

monitor. "I'm sorry. I think I've accidentally scheduled another meeting for this time. I need to pull up my . . . calendar . . . and . . . check, just to be sure," she stammered, looking intently at the screen.

The suggestive melody of "The Stripper" blared from the speakers.

"Surprise! I had the audio on your computer fixed," Mia proclaimed proudly as she left the room.

Patrick stepped behind the desk and leaned over Jacki's shoulder, checking out Mr. Cyberstripper. "So. You had a meeting with another . . . studmuffin. And here I was led to believe I was the only one."

Standing up, she tried to block his view of her computer screen. The music crescendoed. She had to get him out of her office while she still had some semblance of dignity left. Taking his arm, she moved him to the other side of the room and out the door.

While she maneuvered him, she noticed he still wore the same clothes he had on yesterday. And his shirt was wrinkled. And it looked as though he hadn't shaved. Darn the man! Here she was killing herself putting in all these extra hours to save the project, and there he was, out all night partying. She sniffed. It didn't smell like he'd been drinking.

"I brought you a surprise."

"I'm sure you did." Probably a shot glass from the bar down the street, she thought crossly.

"I know I must look like hell, but I was up all night working on a new idea. Can we go back into your office? I left my sketches in there."

"I'll go get them. Meet me in the small conference room."

Patrick nodded. "Mind if I get some coffee first?"

The euphoria of inspiration had left about twenty minutes earlier, and he was going on sheer willpower. The caffeine would help. He was getting too old to pull these all-nighters.

"Long night, Patrick?" Mia handed him a large styrofoam cup of steaming coffee.

"The longest. Thanks." He put in two packets of sugar, a generous splash of creamer, and began to stir. "Mia, what happened to the real cups? I hate these foam things."

Mia threw up her hands. "What can I say? Boss's orders."

"Ready when you are," Jacki called from the conference room.

"Don't touch the sketches until I get there," he answered. "I want to show them to you in the right order." And I want to watch your face when you see them, he thought to himself.

"Is this company going under?" he asked as he entered the room.

"I beg your pardon?"

"It's obvious you can't afford real cups anymore."

"That's a real cup you have in your hand."

"What I'm holding will be around another hundred years after both of us are dead and gone. Don't you know styrofoam's not good for the environment?"

"These cups are environmentally safe and recyclable. Turn it over and read what it says on the bottom. Only, if I were you, I'd wait until it was empty to do that."

"So what was wrong with the real cups?"

"I sent them out to be monogrammed."

"It figures."

Jacki had set the drawings unopened in the center of the table. Patrick picked them up and shook them gently out of the cardboard tube. "I'm sorry I left so abruptly yesterday, but when I get these flashes of inspiration, I have to get them down immediately, or they're lost."

"That was your important business? Why didn't you just stay here and sketch it out? You could have used the conference room."

"I work better alone, without any distractions." And you are definitely a distraction, he added to himself.

"Well, let's see what you've got."

He raised an eyebrow. The caffeine was kicking in.

"Don't look at me like that. You know what I meant. Let's see your drawings."

This might be more difficult than he thought. It could be a hard sell. Why had Winnie picked such an uninspired construction manager? How had she found Ms. Santiago in the first place? In the Yellow Pages, under Cranky People?

He unrolled the first sheet and tacked it up on the wall across from where Jacki was sitting. "I think I've come up with a way for Winnie to have her desert dwelling and her slice of Maine at the same time."

"Go on." She crossed her arms over her chest.

Well, if he expected enthusiasm, this sure wasn't it.

He quickly put up the rest of the drawings and stepped back. "Look for yourself. Start with this one."

Getting out of her seat, Jacki walked over to the

sheet he'd indicated. "A courtyard. This is your idea of inspiration?"

That was it? That was all she had to say about his brainchild?

"It's not just a courtyard. It's an oasis in the desert." Joining her in front of the drawing, his hand caressed the outline of a shape in the center. "See the reflection pool?"

She moved his hand with her pencil. "What's it supposed to be reflecting?"

"The quality of my design."

Instead of the anticipated chuckle, Jacki dissolved into a fit of coughing.

"Hey, lighten up a little. That was a joke. My ego really isn't that big. I meant reflection. As in meditation. Look at the rendering on this next sheet. What do you think now?

"Give me some time here. I need to see all the drawings."

It occurred to Patrick that Jacki could make a fortune playing poker. He couldn't tell what she was thinking. It also occurred to him that maybe he didn't want to know.

She stepped over to the second sheet of paper and cocked her head, tapping the pencil on her chin.

He began to pace, impatiently stabbing his empty foam cup with the stirrer in time with his steps.

Suddenly, she turned around and gave him a dirty look. She tossed her braid over her shoulder and shoved her pencil behind her ear.

He paced the other way.

Jacki walked to the wall where the third drawing was hanging. "This is getting closer. With a little more work, we might have something to begin building. Something that we can get permits for, that is."

This wasn't the response he wanted. She hadn't seen anything yet. Once she saw that final sheet, she'd be totally impressed with him.

"Well, Jacki, you need to see this last drawing. The detail is much better."

Together they stepped in front of sheet number four. And together, they saw it at the same time.

He cringed.

"Yes, that detail is better. In fact, it's even anatomically correct. Almost." Taking the pencil from behind her ear, she put a dot on his X-rated doodle at the bottom of the drawing. "But there should be a mole right about here." The challenge in her eyes was unmistakable.

In one quick motion, he slapped his hand on the paper, covering the female form. When in the world had he drawn that? He knew it had to be him, because no one else had touched the drawings. This was definitely his last all-nighter. She had to think he was some kind of sicko pervert or something. She had to think he wanted to take her clothes off. Which he did, but she didn't have to know about it.

The corner of Jacki's mouth began to twitch. She'd placed her hand over her mouth, but her eyes crinkled with laughter. Watching her, he decided not to fight his own amusement at the situation. He took his hand down from the drawing.

"What can I say? You inspire me."

* * *

The meeting was short, ending with both of them agreeing that Patrick needed to get some much-needed sleep. Jacki accompanied him out to the lobby and watched as he walked down the hall.

After he disappeared from sight, she looked for Mia, finding her sitting on the edge of a desk flirting with one of their young architectural draftsmen.

"Mia, leave Randy alone. I need to talk to you."

"Later, Randy. And don't forget that my birthday is only two weeks away. Make sure it's marked on your calendar. I left my purple pen for you to use when you write it down," Mia chirped, taking several papers with her as she scooted off the desk. She picked them up, placed them in his inbox, and strutted over to where Jacki stood. "What's up, cuz?"

"Is it off yet?"

"What?"

"You know," she lowered her voice, "Mr. Cyber-stripper. Is he gone?"

"Yes. Even though it killed me to do it, the poor man's been evicted. I did it while you and Patrick were in your meeting. But I couldn't stand putting those tasteless trouts and prissy perch back up on your computer. So I found something better for your screensaver."

"Something . . . better?"

"Don't worry. It's G-rated."

"Good thing, because I've had enough X-rated for one day. Please mark my calendar for a meeting with Mr. Godwin tomorrow morning at nine."

"What happened in your meeting today anyway? I thought I actually heard you guys laughing."

"We finally saw eye to eye on something."

"Who knows? Maybe the next meeting you two have you'll end up cheek to cheek."

"Mia! For the last time, this is not one of your romance novels."

"If you say so."

"You know where I am if you need me." As soon as Jacki got back in her office, she was greeted by a row of red chili peppers doing the cha-cha on her computer screen to the Latin beat of "Hot, Hot, Hot."

Once back in his hotel room, Patrick was too wound up to take that nap he'd promised Jacki. The sausage and pepperoni pizza he'd ordered from room service sat half-eaten on a tray on the floor. Stretched out on the bed, his thoughts wandered to the doodles he'd done on the sketch. Did she really have a mole . . . there? Maybe he'd ask her about it. No, better still, maybe he could find out for himself.

Jacki would be a passionate lover. He just knew it. The way she'd laughed at discovering that doodle. The way she moved. The way she flicked her braid over her shoulder when she was angry with him. She did that a lot. She fascinated him. In fact, he hadn't been this intrigued by a woman in years.

Reaching over the side of the bed, he snatched up his sketch pad, grabbed his charcoal pencil, settled back against the pillows, and began to draw. This time, it wasn't Winnie's oasis, but the profile of a woman that began to take shape. Within minutes, Jacki was looking back at him from the paper. He'd drawn her the way he'd like to see her—a

half-lidded stare, full lips parted, and hair slightly
mussed, as though they'd just made love. He sin-
cerely hoped that one day soon, life would imitate
art.

Patrick had just settled back into his chair, legs
stretched up on the drafting table, contentedly stirring his coffee in the real ceramic mug he'd brought
with him, when he thought he heard someone at the
door of the lobby of the J.S. Construction Management Firm. He listened carefully. Yes, he definitely
heard the door rattling. Since it was a Friday evening
and well past quitting time, he was sure that it couldn't
possibly be any of the employees, or even the night
janitor—Curtis had already done his rounds for the
night.

Swinging his legs off the desk, he smiled. It had to
be the pizza delivery person. Zippy Quick Pizza Delivery hadn't come a moment too soon. He was starving. As he made his way down the darkened hall, he
suddenly realized that the Zippy Quick Pizza person
would not be barking. At least not on the job.

He ducked into a nearby closet, leaving the door
only slightly ajar. Peeking out of the closet, what he
saw in the lobby almost made him laugh out loud. A
very large black dog was barking and playfully nip-
ping at Jacki's heels as she boogied to music only she
could hear on her headset. Her luscious hips swayed
irresistibly and her pelvis twisted as she bounced to
the beat of the music. "Ooh, baby, baby," she
crooned into the miniature flashlight on her key

chain. She was making moves even Madonna would envy.

Her incredibly short shorts offered him an extremely pleasant view of a very fine denim-clad backside and legs that seemed to go on forever. As Jacki shimmied and gyrated past him, he could swear her dog was doing a mutt version of the mambo. He held his breath, hoping the animal wouldn't discover him as the dancing duo disappeared into Jacki's office. Patrick stole quietly into his improvised office and softly shut the door.

He was still grinning until his stomach growled. He remembered the extra large double pepperoni pizza that was due to be delivered at any moment. Before that dog got an inkling about what was happening, Patrick had to get to the delivery person. After he took his shoes off, he glanced at his watch. He had no time to waste. He inched open his door and crept out into the hall. Tiptoeing, he made it to Mia's desk and crouched behind it, craning his neck for any dog noises.

He heard the clicking of canine toenails on the tiled part of the lobby floor, and his thighs began to ache from his clandestine position behind the desk. For a moment, he thought about how ludicrous this situation was, and considered giving it up. After all, what was the worst thing that could happen if Jacki found out he was working here at night without her permission? Mia would get in trouble. And the last thing he wanted to do was to be the cause of a family feud.

As the dog looked his way and cocked his ears, Patrick pinned himself closer to the back of the desk and held his breath once again. After what seemed to be an hour, he heard Jacki calling the dog.

"Bart, where are you? Come on back here. You know you're not supposed to wander around without me. We'll only be here a minute. Just until I get that present I forgot. Come on, boy!"

Gratefully, Patrick watched as the dog obediently trotted off in the direction of her voice. Deciding it was now or never, he made a break for the lobby doors just as the pizza delivery guy was stepping out of the elevator. He pulled the young man over to the farthest corner away from the elevator, out of sight from Jacki's office door.

The teenager smiled and tiptoed along with him. "Hey dude, did the boss lady find your hiding spot, or what?" He whispered in a conspiratorial tone.

Patrick was thankful the same person who'd been delivering his pizzas and subs for the last week was a friend of Mia's, sworn to secrecy. "Not yet, Sam, but she happened to come in unexpectedly tonight with her dog, and I've got to tell you, I thought the jig was up." Patrick pulled money out of his wallet and handed it to Sam.

"Bummer. So, do you want me to deliver to another floor next time or something? How about the roof? You know—Operation Pie in the Sky." The teenager winked and nudged Patrick with his elbow.

Patrick had to smile. "That'll work. I'll let you know where to bring it when I call in my next order."

"Great. I'll let my boss know. Later, dude." Handing the pizza box to Patrick, Sam headed down the stairwell.

Patrick carefully scoped out the lobby for any signs

of the giant pooch, and carefully opening the door, began to sneak back to his illicit office space. Unfortunately, Bart waited for him at his door, effectively blocking his path. The dog looked up at him, and spotting the pizza box, began to drool and thump his tail on the carpet.

Patrick quickly opened the box and scooped out a warm slice of double pepperoni pizza. Bart jumped to attention and began wagging his tail so hard it beat the side of his body like a whip. When Patrick offered the piece to him, it was gone in a nanosecond, and the dog's tongue was licking the grease from his palm.

"Good boy," he whispered. "You keep our little secret, and there'll be more pizza for you where this came from."

Wagging his tail, Bart gave him a drooly grin.

Patrick slipped past the contented canine, and, as he was closing his door, gave him one more piece of pizza to seal the deal.

Jacki looked up when Bart came trotting into her office. "Where have you been, big boy?"

He licked his chops in response.

Frowning, Jacki walked over to him and bent down to look more closely at his muzzle. "What have you been eating? You didn't get into Mia's cookies again, did you?"

She couldn't see any crumbs, so maybe the dog was innocent after all. "You have your own treats in here, so you'd better not go scrounging for stuff."

Jacki reached into Bart's treat jar and handed him a doggie biscuit.

Bart held it in his mouth. Walking over to the corner, he set the biscuit down and lay down next to it. He closed his eyes.

She couldn't believe it. Bart never ignored doggie treats unless he had just eaten. And of course, that wasn't possible. Taking Mia's birthday present from its hiding place in the back of her file drawer, she turned off the lights and went home.

SEVEN

Jacki cringed as another wave of sensory overload bombarded her. The casino waitresses' shrieks of "Cocktails! Cocktail delivery!" rang above the jingle and tinkle of coins, the electronic music playing in different keys and rhythms, and the occasional heart-stopping blare of a siren announcing a lucky, screaming winner.

Cigarette smoke, along with every brand of perfume and aftershave imaginable as well as just plain old body odor, assaulted her nostrils. Jacki didn't know whether to put her fingers in her ears or pinch her nose. Flashing lights and strobes and spinning numbers and wall-to-wall video screens competed with the colors of the vivid array of clothing and flashy jewelry. She reached in her purse and pulled out her sunglasses.

A sea of people mumbled to themselves and pushed against each other as they moved from station to station in search of the one machine that would bring them their fortune. And amidst the confusion, Jacki sat on a stool that seemed to be designed for everything but sitting, kicking herself for ever agreeing to let Mia celebrate her twenty-first birthday with an all-day trip to Sunrise Casino.

Jacki had talked Mia into moving to the machines by the window so most of the noise would be behind them instead of surrounding them. She glanced over at Mia to see if she'd run out of coins—or energy—yet. Her cousin's hand was poised in midair, the quarter and the machine temporarily forgotten.

Jacki looked out the window to see what had captured Mia's attention. For a moment she thought it was Roc, her former love interest. Except the man's long, flowing black hair was a couple of shades darker than Roc's. Jacki could catch a glimpse of his one silver earring. His black T-shirt and pants clung to his muscular body like a second skin. The wide leather bands on his wrists drew her attention as he revved the engine on his Harley and motioned to someone.

"If I'd have known this was the view from the machines at the casino, I'd have turned twenty-one a long time ago." Mia commented, her eyes never leaving the scene in front of her. After no reaction from her cousin, she continued, "Jacki, you should seriously consider opening a branch office here. Or at least giving Roc a call so we can look at him every so often. You shouldn't have put all of his photos through the office shredder. Now we don't even have a single shot of him."

Just then, an equally attractive woman climbed on the cycle behind the man they were admiring.

"Jacki, don't you recognize her? She's that dealer from the blackjack table."

"Lucky woman." One of the few things Jacki missed about Roc didn't have anything to do with the man himself, but rather their frequent rides together on his top-of-the-line Harley.

"Don't even think about it. He's very married," a cocktail waitress in a short, tight skirt informed them as she set Jacki's soda in front of her. "They have two really cute little kids."

The three women sighed in unison, two of them for the man, and one for the motorcycle.

"What a waste," Mia lamented.

"You got that right," the waitress agreed as she rearranged the items on her tray. "All the good ones are taken."

"He was okay." Jacki shrugged as she handed the waitress a tip.

" 'Okay'?" Mia yelped. "He was even hotter than Roc. And Roc sizzled."

"Yeah, and Roc was very generous about sharing his sizzle."

"So was Fish Face, and he had no personality and no looks. At least Roc was great to look at. Can't say that about *Señor Pescado.*"

"Mia, we've been over this at least a hundred times. I didn't want to make the same mistake twice, and Evan was as different from Roc as possible. To me, he seemed like the exact opposite. He seemed so . . . safe."

"Yeah, but Evan was obviously making out like a rabbit," Mia reminded her. "And probably with about as much finesse."

Jacki pretended to study the golden Tyrannosaurus rex on the machine in front of her. "I wouldn't know."

The cocktail waitress snorted and moved on to her next customer.

"Mia, stop speculating on Evan's sex life and concentrate on that pig in front of you."

"Hey, Jacki! See that woman with the daisy tattoo on her ankle?" Mia pointed. "You used to have one just like it."

"Mia!" Jacki hissed, "It's rude to point. Put that finger back where it belongs before someone decides to break it off and hand it to you."

"I just wanted you to see that she has a tattoo just like yours."

"I didn't have a tattoo like that one. Mine was smaller. Much, much smaller."

"You shouldn't have had that tattoo removed. I remember now—it was a sunflower. Roc used to call you his 'Little Sunflower.' "

"Look, are we here to celebrate your twenty-first birthday or reminisce about all the monumental mistakes I've made in my love life? If you want a philosophical discussion, we can always go to some place quiet, like the college library. Or we can stop talking about me and teach you how to gamble. What's it going to be, *prima*?"

"Can I have another roll of quarters?"

Several minutes passed, during which Mia dropped coin after coin into the machine, and totally ignored Jacki. For her part, Jacki didn't even want to think about how much money her cousin was feeding the slot machine with the exploding pig.

"Come on, Jacki. You're not playing. You know the old saying: unlucky in love, lucky in cards . . . Well, if that's true, you should be making a killing here."

"Just forget that I'm here, and play your game."

"You know, that's the problem with you, *prima*. Ever since Evan, you've stopped taking a gamble on anything."

Jacki put five quarters into the slot machine with the killer dinosaur motif. And lost. She put in another five, and lost that, too. "Well, third time's the charm," she said cheerily, but the next five coins disappeared just as quickly. Her knees were jammed into the machine. She tried to move the stool back, but with the weighted base, it seemed as if she were moving a ton of bricks.

Finally, she just sat sideways and watched as Mia lost her money.

"Hey, lady, if you're not going to play that machine, give it up to someone who will." A man with a long cigar breathed smoke in her face as he ordered her off the stool. "This place is too crowded for you to waste a machine by just sitting there doing nothing. Now are you going to move, or what?"

Picking up what was left of her small complimentary soda, Jacki stood to search for a chair where she could just sit and shut out this craziness. "Mia, I'm going to find someplace where I can prop my feet up. Are you going to be okay here?"

"Don't worry about me. I'll come find you as soon as I run out of money again."

"I'm sure you will." Jacki gave her a weak smile and trundled off.

The only available chairs that weren't reserved for gambling were at the tiny sandwich stand in the very back of the casino. Settling into the olive green plastic seat, Jacki set her undersized glass on the scarred table and plopped her feet on the empty chair across from her. She closed her eyes.

"Too much partying last night?"

At the sound of the smooth, familiar, baritone voice, Jacki's eyes popped open. Scowling, she whipped off her shades. "You would have more experience in that area than I do, Mr. Godwin."

He sighed. "Jacki, as long as we're here at this horrible casino, can't you find it in your heart to call me Patrick, at least for today? In honor of Mia's birthday, of course."

Sitting up straight, she swung her feet off the chair. "Of course. Okay, in honor of Mia's birthday—Patrick. Since you obviously don't like casinos either, what are you doing here?"

"Same thing you are. Mia asked me to come and help the two of you celebrate her birthday. By the way, I just saw her. She's going for a world record in feeding slot machines."

Jacki shuddered.

He glanced at her glass. "You need a bigger drink. What can I get you?"

"A Pepsi would be nice." Reaching for her purse, she slipped the sunglasses in the side pocket.

"Want something to eat?" He took out his wallet.

"I could use something." She began fumbling in her purse for change.

Patrick shook his head. "My treat. Vegetarian. Right?"

"Right. Nothing with a face. Thanks." She zipped up her purse and set it on the floor beside her feet.

"Stay right there. I'll be back in a minute."

As he stood in line, she took the opportunity to

look at him. It certainly wasn't a hardship. If he just didn't have such poor architectural taste, an obsession for awards, and lousy work habits, he'd be perfect. Oh yes, and the spoon clinking. She shouldn't forget that. Even if he were perfect, she had given up men for the foreseeable future, she decided, picking up her glass and chewing on a piece of the melting ice.

He returned shortly with two sandwiches, an extra large soda, and a cup of coffee for himself. As he poured in the powdered creamer and sugar, picked up his spoon, and started to stir, she put her hand over his. "Don't. Please. Please don't."

"Please don't what?"

"Please don't stir so much. That habit of yours is driving me crazy."

"What habit?"

"You know. That way you have of dumping all of that sugar and white stuff in your coffee—which, by the way, you should be drinking black, without all that junk in it—and clinking and clanking and making all kinds of racket until about an hour later when you've finally decided that everything's dissolved."

"*My* habit is driving you crazy, Ms. Pen-clicker?"

"And exactly what do you mean by that?"

Spotting a cheap plastic pen on the nearby counter, he walked over and picked it up. "Care if I borrow this for a second or two?" After the cashier nodded his consent, Patrick returned to the table, pen in hand.

The minute he sat down, he started clicking the

pen right by her ear. "I can't concentrate when you do this. And you do this all the time."

"That's a flimsy excuse for poor listening skills." Irritated, she grabbed for the pen but latched onto his wrist instead. It was a big mistake. She could feel his muscles tensing against the palm of her hand.

With her free hand, she began to clink his spoon against the side of the coffee cup. "But my clicking is nothing compared to your clinking. It's driving me insane."

"Well, obviously, you don't have too far to go." Gently, but firmly, he clamped his free hand around her wrist. As soon as his fingers touched her arm, it felt as though an electric circuit had been completed. The hair on her arms stood straight up, and there was no way she could control the shiver that started at the base of her spine and spiraled to the top of her head. Even if she wanted to.

Still attached to Patrick, Jacki shot up from her seat and leaned in toward him. She narrowed her eyes. "Get away from me. Leave me alone," she said vehemently.

"I can't. You need to let go of me."

"You let go of me first."

"I already have."

Jacki stomped away before she could embarrass herself any further. Tossing her braid in the air, she walked as far away as possible from the table. Good grief. She could feel the perspiration trickling down her sides as she struggled to regain her composure. She needed to take a deep breath or two. Maybe a hundred. She had to force herself to calm down.

The nerve of the man. Grabbing her in a public

place. It was all she could do to keep from . . . to keep from . . . throwing her arms around him and seeing if his lips tasted as good as they looked. What was wrong with her? The attraction she had once felt for Roc paled in comparison to what she felt now.

There was only one thing to do. Looking around for the ladies' room, she headed for the nearest one and started splashing cold water on her red hot face.

Mia stepped out of a nearby stall. "Jacki! Is there something wrong? Your face is all flushed. Are you okay?"

Ignoring her cousin's concern, Jacki began, "Mia, I have to ask you something important, and it's absolutely imperative that you level with me."

Pumping a generous supply of liquid soap into her hands, Mia rubbed her coin-blackened palms together vigorously. "Well, okay. Shoot." She rinsed off the gray suds, holding her hands out for inspection.

"They still look dirty. You need to scrub them again," Jacki observed, mopping her face with a paper towel. "Tell me the truth, *prima*. Do I have any annoying habits?"

Mia lathered up again. "You sure you want the truth?"

"Absolutely." Jacki wadded up the paper towel and threw it into the already overflowing bin. "I need to know."

Mia reached for a paper towel. "You're always on time."

"That's not a bad habit," Jacki contradicted, peering into the mirror as she smoothed back her hair.

"Well, I think it is." Mia pulled a tube of lipstick from her purse.

Jacki fanned the front of her blouse and wrinkled her nose. "Got any perfume in there? I smell like a cigar."

"Here. Have some Tropical Jungle Musk."

Jacki wasn't sure which smelled worse, the perfume or the cigar, but she dabbed a minute amount on her throat, so as not to hurt her cousin's feelings. "So being on time is my only fault?"

Outlining a perfect tangerine Cupid's bow, Mia held her lips steady as she answered, "You always have to have things your own way."

"That's not a habit. That's genetic," Jacki responded as she applied her vanilla lip gloss.

It seemed to Jacki that Mia took forever to blot her lips before listing the next transgression. "Okay, how about this one? When you're on the phone, you play with the marbles in that big jar on your desk."

"I do?" Jacki didn't remember fiddling with her marble collection, especially while she was on the phone. She'd have to pay closer attention to what she did in the office.

Liberally spraying the Tropical Jungle Musk on her arms, neck and hair, Mia also managed to perfume the woman next to her. "Yeah, but that's not really that annoying."

Smiling an apology, Jacki handed the woman a paper towel. "Is there anything else?"

"Well, there is one thing." Mia leaned in close to the mirror and checked out her dental hygiene.

"What's that?" Jacki looked at her pearly whites, too.

Mia ran her finger across her teeth. "That thing you do with the pen."

"What thing?" Jacki gripped the edge of the vanity. Just in case.

"You know. That pen-clicking thing. You click and click and click and click until I want to scream." Mia demonstrated with her thumb as she spoke.

Letting go of the vanity, Jacki smacked her forehead. "Damn. It's true then."

"Of course it's true. You don't have to beat yourself up. You've been doing it for as long as I can remember. Did someone else mention it?"

Nodding slowly, Jacki headed for the main floor of the casino. "Yes, and I think I owe that someone a great big apology."

Patrick watched Jacki's dramatic exit with a great deal of admiration. The sway of her hips. The way she flipped her hair. He remembered the way her face burned a bright crimson when he touched her. He could actually feel her body temperature rise. There was no mistaking the attraction they felt for each other.

But there was no excuse for his bad behavior. Apparently his habit was just as bad as hers. And he should have figured it out by now since his college roommate was always claiming to have used the last of the coffee. Patrick must have bought three pounds a week throughout his college career, and yet his roommate still swore the canister was empty every time he wanted a cup. Now he knew why.

As much enjoyment as he got from their frequent sparring, he was never going to get anywhere with Jacki as long as they couldn't be together for more than five minutes at a time without going at each other's throats. They definitely needed to call a truce, and he figured he should be the first to suggest it.

There were only two things that could compel Jacki to enter a casino gift shop: boredom and guilt. And she sure as heck wasn't bored. A peace offering. That's what she needed. She walked past the racks loaded with potato chips, chewing gum, candy bars, and cookies, and headed to the glass shelves full of curios and casino keepsakes.

What would Patrick like? A piggy bank with a red pair of dice painted on its side? A back scratcher with the words "Itching To Gamble" inscribed down its length? A deck of only-been-used-once official Sunrise Casino cards? Probably not.

She moved to the next section of items. Wearables. It was hard to envision Patrick in a "Don't Lose Your Pants at Blackjack—Play at Sunrise" T-shirt or a "Born Lucky" baseball cap.

The next aisle held all things glass. She quickly bypassed the "Win Me Over" toothpick holders that were shaped like little toilets. The "Buxom Babe" ashtrays with their unusual cigarette rests and the even tackier shot glasses were also summarily dismissed as gift options. The only things left were the mugs.

What better way to apologize than to offer the very thing she'd wrongly complained about? Now it was just a choice between the black Sunrise Casino and the white poker hand mugs. Except for the lettering, the casino's official mug really wasn't that bad. She figured it would have to do until she had a chance to get a nicer one.

Patrick was on the other side of the gift shop looking for a peace offering of his own. What he really wanted to do was to get Jacki one of those skimpy fire engine red tank tops, but his common sense warned him to choose something safer. He couldn't leave the gift shop without some sort of apology present.

Why hadn't he kept his mouth shut about her and that darned pen? He picked up a wooden rose. It looked so real. Holding it to his nose, he breathed in deeply and grimaced. That rose might look real, but it smelled like the cedar chips he kept in his closet back in Maine.

It was then that he found the perfect gift. There, on the middle shelf of the middle aisle, sat dozens of containers of pens. One of the clear, round canisters was labeled, "Turn me over." Patrick figured it didn't mean that he should dump the contents. Picking up a purple pen featuring a bikini-clad female, he did just what the sign said. The bikini was history. Chuckling, he turned the pen over and over, dressing and undressing her again, all the while marveling at the wonders of modern technology.

"Having fun entertaining yourself?"

He knew that voice.

Turning around, he smiled at his former nemesis. "Hello, Jacki. I think I've just found the perfect date for Mr. Cyberstripper . . ."

"And unfortunately, a perfect present for Mia . . ."

"Great idea, but you'd better be the one to give it to her."

"We don't want her getting any ideas."

"Any more than she already has," he agreed. He reached for a plain gold pen. "How about this one for you? I see that it comes with a guarantee against breaking, so you can click to your heart's delight."

Jacki held out the mug she'd chosen for him. "And you can clink as much as you want."

"We're quite a pair, aren't we?"

"That we are."

EIGHT

"I'm here to see Jacqueline."

Mia glared at the tall, lean man standing in front of her desk. "Go away, Evan. You know you're not welcome here."

"Hello to you, too, Cousin Mia." His smirk accentuated his thin lips.

"I'm not related to you now, tomorrow, or ever," Mia hissed as she rose from her chair. "You may call me Ms. Alvarez. Better yet, leave the office immediately and don't call me anything."

"Rude, as always." Evan rolled his eyes upward. "Some things never change."

"And you're still the biggest creep I've ever met. Some things never change."

"I'm not here to talk with you . . ." he began.

She gave a loud snort. "Thank goodness."

Ignoring her reaction, he started toward the hall. "I'm here to see Jacqueline."

Mia moved between Evan and the entrance to the hallway. "You can't see Jacki. My cousin isn't here. She's away on vacation."

"Then why is her car in the parking lot?" His eyes narrowed suspiciously.

"She loaned it to me while she was gone."

"I don't believe you. Jacqueline would never trust anyone with that precious Cherokee of hers."

"Then believe this, *cabrón. Tú tienes los morales de un perro de las calles.*"

"I suppose I should warn you—I understand every word you're saying." Evan smirked. "I minored in Spanish."

"Well, just in case you missed a word, let me tell you in English. You have the morals of a street dog."

"Look, amusing as this is, I didn't come here to be insulted by you. I need to talk to Jacqueline. We have something urgently important to discuss."

"Over my dead body."

"That can be arranged." Evan shoved past her and marched down the hall to Jacki's office.

Mia was right on his heels. "I'm sorry, Jacki," she apologized as she skidded into the office behind Evan. "I wasn't able to stop old Fish Face from coming in. Do you want me to call security?"

Jacki looked up from her desk and stared at the intruder. Were his eyes always that shifty? What in the world had she ever seen in this man, a full-time, practicing sleazeball? Her brain cells must have been on strike or something. "No, Mia. I'll be okay. You can leave us alone."

"Hello, Jacqueline."

Just hearing Evan's voice again made Jacki's stomach turn and her fingernails ache, but she'd die before she let him know how much he affected her. "What do you want?" She hoped she sounded as disgusted as she felt. "Make this brief, Evan, or I'll take Mia up on that offer to call security."

"Your cousin's rude and interfering, the same as always," he sneered. "I never did like her."

Jacki crossed her arms in front of herself. "You can be sure the feeling's mutual."

"I'm not here to talk about that obnoxious relative of yours, Jacqueline. I'm here because I made a mistake. A big one."

Shaking her head, Jacki contradicted him. "I don't think it was a mistake that you married Allison instead of me. The two of you deserve each other."

"Of course our marriage isn't a mistake." He rolled his eyes. Jacki wished they would freeze in that position, he did it so often. "My mistake was buying the discount tickets for that honeymoon cruise you and I were supposed to take so far in advance that I can't get a refund."

She shrugged. "So take your wife on the cruise."

Giving an exaggerated sigh of exasperation, he continued. "It's been three months, but Allison still has morning sickness. And the tickets expire next week."

"That's your problem."

"No, it's our problem. Yours and mine. I'm sitting here with non-refundable, non-transferable, about to expire cruise tickets, and I refuse to eat the loss. After all, I bought them for both of us. For our honeymoon."

"Which fortunately, we didn't have. I still don't get your point."

"I want you to pay for your half."

"You what?"

"I want you to pay for your half of the tickets." He took a small, white piece of paper from his pocket and carefully unfolded it. Jacki recognized it immediately as a length of adding machine tape. It figured.

"Let's see." Evan appeared to study whatever he'd written. "The total cost of the cruise for both of us was three thousand, seven hundred, eighty-three dollars and sixty-nine cents. That brings your share of the bill to one thousand, eight hundred, ninety-one dollars and eighty-five cents."

A third voice rang out from across the room. "You aren't even going to pay the extra penny?" Jacki hadn't noticed Patrick coming in, and she had no idea how long he'd been standing in the doorway.

"Hello, Jacki." Patrick's voice was as smooth as the truffle filling in a fine European chocolate. "I take it this is the old boyfriend."

"Ex-fiancé. I'm the ex-fiancé."

"Ex-fiancé?" The two men stared at each other for several seconds, then Patrick looked at Jacki in amazement. "You were actually engaged to this guy?"

Jacki put her hands in the air, palms up, and nodded. "I'm afraid so."

"I see." Patrick turned to Evan. "Mia tells me you're a very educated man. With a B.A."

"That's right. Summa cum laude."

"And an M.B.A."

"Harvard Business School. Top five percent of my class."

"And you're also a C.P.A."

"Passed the test first time."

"You must be a real smart guy."

Evan beamed proudly. "That's what they tell me."

"Ever take philosophy?"

"I didn't need to. It wasn't applicable to my career field. Why?"

"Because I have a philosophical question for you. A smart guy like you shouldn't have any trouble at all answering it."

"Shoot."

Patrick took a step toward Evan. "If you—accidentally—fell out of this twelfth story window"—taking another step forward, he looked meaningfully over Evan's shoulder—"and there was no one below to hear you, would the screams you made on the way down really make noise?"

"Jacqueline, this man's dangerous," Evan declared in a loud whisper. He glanced down as if to verify the enormous distance between Jacki's office and ground level.

An evil grin split her face. "I certainly hope so." She could actually see sweat beading on Evan's upper lip. It was the best thing she'd seen in a long, long time.

"I suggest you leave right now if you intend to exit by way of the door." Patrick took one more step toward Evan. "Oh, and by the way, if you ever feel the urge to bother Ms. Santiago again, think about our little lesson in philosophy first."

The man darted around him and scurried out of the room faster than a rat on the *Titanic*.

"What all did you hear?" Jacki's eyes filled with admiration for the man who had actually made Evan flee.

Patrick gave her a crooked grin. "Enough. That guy's really a piece of work, isn't he?"

"He sure is. I can see now that our breakup was

the best thing that ever happened to me." She raised an eyebrow. "So, Patrick, would you really have done it?"

He was a vision of innocence. "Really have done what?"

"Thrown him out the window."

Patrick chuckled. "I don't believe in violence, Jacki. Usually."

"Hold that elevator!" Jacki raced to the closing door, Bart leading the way. As she jumped inside, she almost ran into a delivery person holding a greasy white bag in one hand and balancing an extra large drink cup in the other. Catching herself before she flattened the teenager against the elevator wall, she managed to step on Bart's tail and the young man's foot at the same time.

"Oh, gosh. I'm so sorry—it's just that on Sundays, only one elevator works, and if you don't catch it when you see it, it takes a million years before it ever comes—" Jacki stopped in midsentence. The delivery person didn't seem to be even remotely interested in her apology. Of course, it was hard to listen when a hundred and twenty pound dog was standing with his front paws on your shoulders and his head stuffed into the bag you were holding.

"Hey, lady, can you get your dog down?" The young man's eyes looked as though they were about to pop out of his head.

She threw down her briefcase and grabbed Bart's front legs, pushing his huge paws back onto the floor.

"Sit, boy." Her fingers grasped his collar and Bart

sat. Longingly, he gazed at the paper bag, panting eagerly. The delivery boy clutched the torn, wet bag and moved into the farthest corner of the elevator.

She adjusted her shoulder bag, which had slipped during her wrestling match with her huge pet. "We owe you an apology. He gets really excited around food." Jacki looked down at Bart and shook her head. "Is it ruined? I'll pay for it. I really am sorry he did this."

"It'll probably be okay." The teenager opened the bag and surveyed the damage. "We wrap all of our subs with plastic wrap. It looks like he only messed up the napkins on top. The guy who ordered these probably won't even notice."

Jacki wasn't sure she wanted to know a man who wouldn't notice dog drool on his food. "Well, if you're sure . . ." She bent over and picked up her briefcase, maintaining a firm hold on the collar. Bart seemed to be sulking.

"It's okay. I'm sure," he repeated, keeping an eye on the dog. He had squeezed even further into the corner, if that was possible.

"Bart won't hurt you," she assured him. "He's just a big, lovable old teddy bear."

"More like a grizzly bear," the teenager muttered.

Jacki prayed for the elevator to open. She knew Bart's self-control would only last for a few more seconds. She could feel his muscles tensing already. Finally, the elevator stopped on the twelfth floor, and Jacki literally leaped out, dragging her reluctant pet with her.

Only they weren't alone. The delivery guy had

come with them, and was keeping a safe distance behind. "He's kind of a big dog, isn't he?"

The young man obviously hadn't learned his lesson. He was swinging the paper bag at his side as he
walked, making it a prime target at Bart's eye level.

She struggled to keep Bart under her control.
"He's a Labrador, but he thinks he's a lap dog. He's
generally harmless."

"Generally harmless?" the teenager gulped.

"Except where food is concerned. He's been
known to jump over a six foot fence and steal a siz-
zling steak off a neighbor's barbecue grill, and then
jump back and pretend that nothing happened.
Which I believed, until I found the steak bone hidden
in my bed."

As she arrived at her office lobby door, she juggled
her briefcase and Bart's collar in order to get the key
chain from her shoulder bag. Out of the corner of
her eye, she noticed the delivery guy standing silently,
watching her. She turned to him. "Can I help you
find the office you need?"

"Do you work *here?*" The young man shifted his
feet.

"Yes." She finally fished out the key and slid it into
the lock. The reassuring click had Bart shoving the
door open. She let him run into the darkened lobby.
When she turned to ask the teenager where he was
supposed to go, he was gone. "Great. He's probably
a homicidal maniac," she grumbled to herself.

Once inside the lobby, she flicked on the lights.
Bart was nowhere to be found, although she had a
pretty good idea where he might be. She headed for
her office and the doggie treat jar, his favorite spot

in the building. However, she stopped before she got there. Bart was down the opposite hall, his nose glued to the bottom of the storage room door, sniffing so loudly she could hear him several yards away.

"Bart! What in the world are you doing?" Shaking her head, she trudged into her office to deposit her purse and briefcase. Bart had probably found some nasty rodent, or worse yet, a cockroach, and he wouldn't give up the hunt until he had it cornered— and dead.

She reached for the treat jar, hopeful that she could cajole him back into her office, where she could close the door and keep him from harassing the entire vermin population of Phoenix. Stepping out of her office, she rattled the treat jar. "Look what I have for you! Your favorite snack!"

Nose flattened against the door, Bart continued with his canine vacuum trick.

Taking a few more steps, she shook the jar again. "Come on, you know you love them. Yummy, yummy."

The dog looked at her once, whined, and began to dig the carpet at the bottom of the door with his paws.

Racing down the hall, she yelled, "Bart, you stop that this minute. That's a brand-new carpet!"

Bart stopped and sat.

She looked at him.

He looked at her.

What had gotten into him? Except for stealing Mia's cookies, he was usually well-behaved when she brought him to the office. She stroked his head as she squatted down to his level. "What have you found, boy? Rats? Roaches?"

Bart sniffed the door one more time.

"Okay, I'll call the exterminator in the morning. Now come on!"

Bart refused to budge.

Getting behind him, she gave his one hundred and twenty pound rump a shove. It was like trying to move a mountain.

Jacki grabbed his collar. He began to whine and dig at the carpet again.

"You are the most stubborn animal! Okay, I'm going to prove to you there's nothing behind this door."

She stood and reached for the knob.

Bart began to prance and bark.

"Settle down. There are no rats in the storage room."

She flung the door open wide.

There, sitting at an old drafting table—make that *her* old drafting table—was none other than Patrick Godwin in the flesh. Her former storage room had been transformed into a makeshift architectural studio . . . without her permission. Her eyes flashed in anger.

"Well, well, well, Bart boy, I apologize. I was wrong. You did smell a rat in the storage room. A big one." She put her hands on her hips. "Hello, Patrick. Nice setup."

He held up his hands in surrender. "Guess I'm busted."

He knew he was seeing the other extreme of her anger. Glacial in its impact, her eyes cold as emeralds.

"I can explain."

"Please do. Breaking. Entering. Staying. Where do

you want to start?" Stepping over a stack of empty pizza boxes, she pulled up a battered chair and sat down.

Patrick sighed. He felt like the world's biggest fool. Why had he let Mia talk him into borrowing that darned key? He should have taken the time to find someplace else to work. But no, he'd been too anxious to start the redesign of the Longmont project.

"Are you sure you have time to hear this? It could take a while . . ."

"I'm all ears." Bart put his head on her lap and looked up as though he were listening, too.

For one of the few times in his life, Patrick was at a loss for words. He did know that there was no way he'd drag Mia into this, even if she had been his accomplice. "I needed someplace to draw."

"That's it?" Jacki spread out her arms in disbelief. "You needed someplace to draw?"

"That's it." He felt his face flush with guilt.

"So why didn't you just ask?"

He shrugged.

"I don't understand how you got in without someone noticing." He could hear the resignation creep into her voice.

"I came back here before everyone went home for the evening."

"And stayed."

"And stayed."

There was a long, uncomfortable silence. The disappointment on her face made him long for the anger that had been there only moments before.

"Look, I don't care whether or not you use this room," she told him in a flat voice. "In fact, if you'd asked, I would have given you a cubicle of your own. Just don't sneak around and lie to me. I've had enough of lying, sneaking men to last me several lifetimes."

Before Patrick could respond, Jacki turned on her heel and left, dog in tow.

NINE

Despite the heat, the next two weeks felt cold and empty to Patrick. Jacki barely said a word to him except to criticize his blueprints or to get clarification on a plan detail. On this particular day, she had broken her code of silence to leave him a message at the hotel. Their building permit had been issued and she wanted a meeting to finalize the interior finishes.

Jacki was seated at her drafting table, intently studying the most recent set of approved plans. Her long hair was plaited in its usual single braid. A few curls had escaped where she had run her hand through her hair in frustration. The sun from the window behind her made her look as though she glowed all over. Jacki glanced up at Patrick with a look of disgust on her face when he came in.

"Well, Patrick, we've got our backs up against another deadline, and you're twenty-three minutes late. You were late yesterday, too."

"Only five minutes. I was almost half an hour early on Monday."

"That doesn't count. We don't bank time around here, especially when the schedule starts to slip. And this one is definitely slipping. Today we need to make final decisions on tile selections, wall coverings, bathroom fixtures, and luminares," Jacki said firmly, consulting the project timelines which now covered nearly every square inch of the wall on her left. "I need to order them immediately."

She clicked her pen, waiting for a response. He was mesmerized by the shimmering highlights of her hair. He was particularly fascinated by the wayward wisps that framed her face. He wondered if he'd ever see her smile again.

She clicked her pen.

"Look, Patrick, you've got to make some decisions," she insisted. "Either you design the best house you can for Winnie, or you design something unlivable to get your award. Which is it going to be? I assure you I want no part in the latter. Remember, I have a reputation to maintain, too," she advised him coolly.

The frosty tone of her voice drew his attention from her intriguing physical attributes. He was still silent as she continued. "We don't have a lot of time, so you're going to have to think fast and decide. The contractor is ready to proceed. I need some direction here. Are you listening? Would you pay attention? We don't have time for daydreaming."

"Excuse me? You need direction? *You?* Giving direction seems to be your specialty. You've forced me into changing everything from the roof to the landscape plans."

Jacki stood up, her fists clenched at her sides. "For the past few weeks, you've been doing nothing but trying to force me to accept your architectural suggestions, no matter how expensive, unworkable, or just plain stupid they are."

"Stupid?" he sputtered. "My ideas are . . . stupid?"

"Well, some of them are." She started clicking the pen faster. "Now, when I really need to know what you want, you refuse to give me a straight answer. In fact, you refuse to give me any answer at all. For the last time, a decision has to be made on the interior design of Winnie's house. We're running out of lead time to order whatever materials you select. Do you want the house to stand empty for a year because you can't decide what kind of faucet to put in the bathroom?"

He didn't answer.

"Well, do you?"

Patrick seethed inwardly. He'd be damned if he'd give her the interior plans he'd been working so hard on the last few days. Just let her think that his first effort was the final one.

"Stop acting like a typical hoity-toity architect, and make some decisions to make this house functional." Jacki's voice rose to a higher pitch.

Privately, Patrick knew he had put off lots of decisions about hardware and finishes, but this was a matter of principle. Jacki was being just plain obnoxious. "So now I'm a typical hoity-toity architect. Something tells me we're not on the same team anymore."

She took another step forward. "Did Winnie tell you something I missed here? Your conceptual interior design scheme is, at the very best, garage sale Western. You've been in Phoenix more than five weeks now, Mr. Godwin. How many cactus spine lamps with rawhide-laced desert scene shades have you noticed? Have you sat in a lot of cattle horn chairs? Have you seen even one wagon wheel chandelier?"

"Well, no, but . . ."

Jacki was on a roll. "And stuffed animals—dead stuffed animals on every wall? Hundreds of dead, beady little eyes staring at you. Dead deer. Dead elk. Dead—"

"I don't think a vegetarian's view of taxidermy is exactly unbiased. I was simply trying to create an ambiance. An atmosphere. An experience. One that would most advantageously set off Winnie's—"

Jacki interrupted. "Winnie's what? Her dead Bambi collection?"

Patrick's blue eyes turned flinty as his voice lowered to a level more controlled, much more deadly. "You've crossed the line here, Jacki." He lifted a hand in warning. "If you were a man, I'd ask you to step outside."

"And if you were a man, Mr. Godwin, you wouldn't act like some wimpy, out-of-touch architect. If you were a man, you'd make your decisions based on what you know is right, not to win an award," Jacki said, punctuating each sentence by poking his chest with her index finger. "You'd make those decisions now, and the project could move forward again."

Patrick glared at her, clearly furious. "If I were a man, Ms. Santiago, I wouldn't tolerate your insults."

He took a long step forward. Their bodies almost touched. She backed away, taking heed of the dangerous glint in his eyes.

He stepped forward again.

She stepped back.

They continued this strange almost-dance until the back of her legs touched her desk, and the front of her legs were pressed snugly against his hard, muscular thighs.

"Since I am a man, Ms. Santiago, I can find more effective ways of silencing you."

Her eyes widened as he bent forward and gave her an electrifying kiss that would have knocked her socks off, had she been wearing any. His lips were warm, firm, and demanding. The kiss scorched her mouth with its intensity. She closed her eyes and made a small noise in the back of her throat. He pressed her closer. This felt even better. His hands began to stroke her back. Delicious shivers went up and down her spine as her body responded to his sensual assault.

The loud, shrill ringing of the phone signaled an abrupt return to reality.

Patrick looked at Jacki with a bemused expression.

The phone kept ringing.

Taking a steady breath, she put her hands against his chest and determinedly pushed him away, hating the powerful attraction to him that she couldn't help but feel.

Her voice quivered as she looked directly at him. "Mr. Godwin, you might be able to get away with behavior like this in Maine, but in this state, we have laws against sexual harassment. Please leave my office immediately, or I will have you thrown out."

"Don't bother. I've never forced myself on a woman in my life, and I certainly don't intend to start now."

Her Diego Rivera print crashed to the floor as the door slammed behind him.

"That woman is—impossible," Patrick ground out as he stalked past Mia's desk.

Dropping her newest favorite romance novel, Mia ran down the hall and began yelling before she hit the office door. "Jacki! What in the world did you do to poor old Patrick this time? I can't leave you two alone for one minute!"

Jacki, seated at the drafting table, held her head in both hands and looked decidedly dazed. "Not that it's any of your business, which it isn't, *prima*. But he did something terrible to me."

"Patrick couldn't be terrible if he tried."

"Oh, yes he could," Jacki contradicted.

"Yes, and exactly what crime against mankind did our hunk commit?" Mia asked, her face mirroring her skepticism.

"Patrick . . . Patrick . . . well, Patrick made improper advances."

"Excuse me. Improper what? What do you mean? Spit it out."

Jacki sighed and put her head back down in her hands. "He kissed me," she whispered in a strangled voice.

"He kissed you? The nerve. I can't believe it. So what was it like? He looks like he'd be one great kisser! Details, I want details!"

Jacki narrowed her eyes. "Mia . . ." she warned.

"Did you kiss him back? Did anyone see you two? Why is it that everything exciting happens when I'm not there?"

Jacki groaned as she eased herself from her chair.

"You were here when he organized the basketball game in our office lobby that first day," she reminded her. "In fact, if I remember correctly, you were the one standing on the counter trying to make a basket."

"I'm talking the good stuff here, not sports. Lord, you look pale. He didn't hurt you, did he?" Mia put her arm around Jacki's shoulder.

"Of course I'm not hurt," Jacki snapped, shrugging off Mia's arm. "Will you just leave it alone?"

A very long silence followed Jacki's outburst.

"Now I suppose you're going to yell at me for giving him the key."

"What key?"

"The one to the office."

"*You* let him in?"

Much to her chagrin, Mia's eyes welled with tears. She sniffed loudly. "I just wanted you to live happily ever after, like they do in romances. I wasn't trying to interfere. Honest."

Mia looked like a hurt puppy.

Jacki felt like the world's biggest jerk. "Oh, *prima*, I'm really sorry."

"Don't worry, Jacki. I'll always like you. No matter what, you're still my cousin." Mia gave one more good, hard sniff.

As Jacki comforted her, she knew she'd have to apologize to Patrick. Again.

TEN

Jacki couldn't believe her eyes. There, in the middle of the desert, at the end of the dusty, almost nonexistent road, sat a motorcycle. At first, suspicious that some hooligan was trespassing on Winnie's property, she turned off the ignition of her Cherokee and coasted quietly until she was behind the big bike. Walking up to it, she glanced around, hoping that the owner wouldn't see her. She ran her hand over the sun-warmed leather of the motorcycle seat. Gingerly, she touched the glistening chrome handlebars, expecting to be burned by hot metal. The bike must not have been there very long—the sun hadn't turned the chrome red hot yet.

The motorcycle was brand-new. Its luscious red enamel gleamed in the sunshine. She wished she could ride it.

An idea occurred to her. It couldn't be Patrick's, could it? A delicious thought. Who else would be out here? Except maybe a serial killer with really great taste in motorcycles. A chill went down her spine. She wasn't sure whether to be terrified or thrilled.

"Go ahead. Try it out."

She jumped, nearly knocking the bike over. They

grabbed for it at the same time. For the life of her, she couldn't figure out how Patrick had managed to sneak up on her, but there he was.

"Is this yours?" Her fingers caressed the leather seat once more.

"Hot off the showroom floor," he said. He shot her a look that made her knees melt.

He was making her nervous. A trail of perspiration trickled down the side of her cheek. Untying his bandanna, he offered it to her.

She dabbed at her face. His spicy scent lingered on the blue fabric.

"That's some bike. First time out?"

"First time out," he confirmed.

Aha. Just as she'd thought. "How does it ride?"

"Smooth. Real smooth. Want to go for a spin?" He grinned at her hesitation. "I know you want to."

"Patrick, I'd love to, but I have to clear something up first. Mia told me about the key. I treated you so unfairly . . ."

"She's not in trouble, is she?"

"No."

"Then there's no problem." He shrugged. "Stop worrying about it, and let's go."

"There's only one helmet."

In one fluid motion, he mounted the bike and tossed her the helmet. "You take it. We won't go very far."

"Are you sure you know how to drive one of these?"

His raised eyebrow dared her to doubt him. "Hop on." He turned on the ignition. "You'll know soon enough."

Fastening the helmet, she straddled the seat behind him. As he revved the engine, the bike lurched forward. She had no choice but to grab his waist and hang on, hooking her thumbs around his belt.

Patrick grinned and tightened his grip on the handlebars. There was only one thing better than sailing along with the wind whipping all around you, and that was sailing along with the wind whipping all around you while a gorgeous female clung to your body. He could feel her heart speed up as he accelerated.

So the businesslike Ms. Santiago liked her recreation fast and dangerous. The woman not only intrigued him, she excited him. He accelerated again, chuckling as she made a noise deep in her throat, grabbed the front of his shirt, and pressed her legs even closer to his. As her soft curves molded to the contours of his hard, muscular body, he felt a surge of wanting so powerful he could think of nothing else.

The few minutes on the bike seemed more like a few seconds. Somewhere in his passion-fogged mind, he remembered his promise to her that the ride would be short. Patrick sighed as he fishtailed to a stop.

Jacki didn't want the ride to end. "Why don't we go over to the ridge that overlooks Winnie's property?" she yelled over the roar of the engine, pointing to a rise in the distance. "Just be sure not to get too close to the edge. The ground out here in the desert can be crumbly and unstable."

Nodding, he took off in the direction she indicated and stopped a few yards away from the edge of the ridge. He turned off the engine and reluctantly waited for Jacki to peel herself from his body, which she did more quickly than he liked.

Jacki stood in the patchy shade of a palo verde tree fanning the front of her blouse, bringing the motion to an abrupt halt when she noticed that he was watching her every movement with great interest. She headed for the edge of the ridge. He followed.

Not noticing that she had stopped, Patrick plowed into her, thrusting her forward to the very edge. She twisted her body as the ground literally began to crumble and give way underneath their feet.

He grabbed her waist and pulled hard. There was little or no traction on the fine dust of the desert floor. He lurched several feet backwards, dragging her against him. They stood there, frozen together. His chest heaved, not so much from exertion, but from an effort to keep his burgeoning desire under control.

Jacki's soft sigh tickled his ear. He felt her breathing, rapid and irregular. So the untouchable Ms. Santiago was affected by this, too. The heat of the day enhanced the aroma of her perfume. The scent of her hair was unique. Floral. Sweet. Delicious. He could smell the coconut sunscreen lotion on the side of her neck. Even with his eyes closed, his senses were overwhelmed by Jacki's nearness and nothing else.

Jacki was certain if she stood there much longer, she would burst into flame, a victim of the spontaneous combustion of passion. The two of them made a motionless tableau, neither one wanting to make the next move.

She felt as though someone had knocked the air out of her lungs. Jacki had never been so aware of anyone in her life as she was of Patrick at this very moment.

When she could finally breathe again, she tried to take a deep, steadying breath, but his spicy scent sent shivers down the length of her body.

They were still only inches away from each other. She couldn't tear her gaze away from him. It would be so easy . . .

Patrick watched as Jacki studied him. He saw her features soften and her pupils dilate with desire. His lips curved in a satisfied smile at the knowledge that she wanted him as badly as he wanted her.

Stepping forward, he clasped her body closer to his. Claiming her lips, he crushed her to him. Their kiss was urgent, demanding. Consumed by the need to touch her, he skimmed his hands slowly downward. Her eager response matched his.

Then, just as quickly, he watched her bank her attraction as the sound of catcalls interrupted their mutual obsession.

"Look," she croaked.

There, in the valley below them, stood the entire construction crew for the Longmont project, each one of them giving the two of them their full and undivided attention.

When she turned her back and raced to the bike, Patrick was only sorry that she hadn't stuck around to see all six men giving him a thumbs-up.

By the time they'd reached the superintendent's construction trailer, Jacki was pretty sure her color was back to normal. She introduced the two men to each other.

Mike Carpenter, a tall, wiry man in his late thirties, took a cigarette from the pack in his shirt pocket.

Jacki put her hand on his arm. "Mike, you know how I feel about smoking."

"Okay, you're the boss." Good-naturedly, he stuck the cigarette behind his ear. "Saw you guys up on the ridge," he grinned. "Pretty dangerous up there, isn't it?"

"Well, it can be if a man doesn't know how to handle it," Patrick responded as Jacki felt her face redden with embarrassment.

"I guess you know how to handle it then."

"I'm learning."

Jacki choked, trying to figure out which man to kill first. Definitely Patrick. She needed Mike on the jobsite. But after the house was done, he would be fair game too . . .

Mike, probably unaware that his life was in danger, led the way into the trailer.

"We've got a lot of work ahead of us. We just got the permits today." She was anxious to be somewhere that she didn't have to look at the dumb ridge.

"Mia faxed me some of the stuff. Looks good. Except with all the patio walls, it looks like we're going to need a mason now. I'd better start getting bids. I still need the specs for the interiors. Have you guys finished that yet? You know that if you're still thinking about using wood floors, those take three or four months to get here."

Patrick nodded. "As a matter of fact, we're meeting

tonight to finalize the interiors. We can order the flooring sometime tomorrow morning."

"We're having a meeting?"

"Yes, don't you remember? Eight o'clock."

"Eight o'clock?" She frowned.

"Too late for you? Do you have a problem with burning the midnight oil?"

The nerve of the man. She'd worked practically every night until midnight since they started this project. "Eight o'clock is perfect."

Jacki decided to go home and take a swim before their evening meeting. By the time she got home, it was late afternoon, and the pool was in the shade of the house. The motion of the water calmed her. As her foot dangled over the side of the raft, the ripples caressed her ankle. After a few minutes, languid as she was, she still wasn't able to fully unwind. Bart, who as usual had no trouble at all relaxing, had climbed out of the pool and was snoring on the warm patio deck.

As she rolled over to her stomach and trailed her hand in the water, she couldn't stop thinking about Patrick. He'd sure surprised her when he announced to Mike that the interior specifications would be done by the morning. And what about that eight o'clock meeting? The man mystified her.

She wondered what would have happened earlier in the day if she and Patrick hadn't had an audience. Her body quivered at the thought. And now they were going to be working closely together—maybe all night. Alone. It could prove to be very interesting.

* * *

Patrick played hooky that afternoon, too. Back in his hotel room, he landed on the bed, exhausted. He hoped the kid in charge of valet parking had taken good care of his new wheels. After all, he planned on using it a lot from now on, especially in the company of one tall, green-eyed female. He had no idea a ride on a motorcycle could be so, uh, exhilarating. He wondered if Jacki thought about him the same way he thought about her. The very idea made him moan.

But now he was in no condition to even think about doing anything. In fact, he was so tired he was afraid he might not wake up in time for the meeting he had called for eight o'clock that night. Groaning, he reached over and left a request for a wake-up call in four hours.

The phone call came sooner than he wanted. Hanging up on the annoying automated message, he struggled out of bed and headed straight for the shower. Maybe the water would help clear his head.

The water didn't help, but he hoped the food he'd bought would. That evening, Patrick came into Jacki's office carrying several cartons of Chinese take-out. He plopped them on the table.

"What have you got there?"

"Sweet and sour pork and Mongolian beef."

She grimaced.

"And a couple of faceless dishes for my favorite vegetarian."

Smiling with delight, she opened the cartons and selected tofu stir fry and brown rice. "Perfect! I have forks in the kitchen."

"I thought we'd try these instead." He handed her a pair of chopsticks.

"I've never used chopsticks before."

"There's always a first time for everything. Let me show you how to hold them."

For one of the few times in her life, Jacki forgot about the food in front of her as Patrick arranged her fingers on the chopsticks. Her hand trembled. He kept his hand on hers and guided the chopsticks to the food. She'd never look at Chinese food the same way again.

Gently, he squeezed her fingers together over a piece of tofu. As soon as they lifted the slippery morsel out, it slid back into the carton. They tried again. His hand was warm and callused, a sharp contrast to the cool, smooth plastic of the chopsticks.

Jacki didn't care if it took all night to get the chopsticks to work. She was enjoying this. Much to her disappointment, she finally got the hang of it, even if she did have to bend so close to the carton her face was nearly in the soy sauce.

In the background, the familiar drone of Curtis vacuuming the lobby carpet reminded her that they weren't alone.

"So how long have you been an architect?"

"Since I was born." He helped himself to another serving of the Mongolian beef.

She laughed. "So instead of being born with a silver spoon, it was a silver drafting pencil?"

"Well, almost. I always preferred Legos to Little

League. It drove my father crazy. My parents had wanted enough kids for a baseball team, but only ended up with me and my sister."

"You have a sister?"

"An older, bossier one."

"A good woman."

"The best. Maggie's got three kids and runs her own restaurant."

"I don't have any brothers or sisters, but I sort of inherited my cousin Mia." She wiped her mouth with a napkin. "Keeping up with her is a full-time job."

He laughed sympathetically. "How long have you been in construction?"

"My dad died and left me this business about four years ago, but I worked for him since I got out of high school."

"You must have learned well. Your company has a really great reputation."

His praise pleased her. "I have good people working for me. But we need to be better than good on this project. What about the article Winnie wants in that architectural journal? And what about that award she's got her heart set on? It bothers me that she's expecting our project to get that kind of recognition."

"That's exactly what I told her. Awards and recognitions aren't sure things. They never are. I think if it happens, it happens—and I'll try my damnedest to make it happen—but it can't be our main goal."

She poked at another piece of tofu. "I know plenty of architects who design with glory in mind and give no thought to what the owner needs. And there are architects out there who would sell their souls just to get mentions in the journals. Awards are nice, but I can show you houses around here that have won all kinds of honors and aren't fit to live in." Spearing the tofu with the chopstick, she finally took a hard-earned bite.

"One prestigious award like the Mitchell Burrell Medallion can make the difference between a new firm succeeding or closing its doors."

"And you have a new firm?"

"You bet I do." He popped open their cans of soda and handed one of them to her. "I was with a large, established group of architects, but all of their projects were beginning to look alike."

"Cookie cutter designs?"

"You've got that right. And I wanted every one of my buildings to be unique. So I left and struck out on my own."

"What are you going to do if you don't get your medallion?"

"There are no ifs involved, Jacki. I have to get it."

When the last grain of rice disappeared, Patrick got up and cleared the table. She watched as he threw the chopsticks into the trash can. She'd take them out later, but he didn't need to know it.

"Let's get down to business," Jacki suggested.

They went to the adjoining drafting room. She turned on both computers. "Life is so much easier with automated specification charts."

"Amen." Patrick loaded a disk into the drive of the computer. "Here. Take a look at this revised list of hardware fixtures."

Jacki scanned the screen. "This is much, much better." She nodded her approval. "This should also be closer to our projected budget than that other stuff you proposed. Now, if you'll let me borrow that disk, while you're finalizing quantities, I'll start estimating costs."

The custodian knocked a couple of times on the door, and opened it. "See you finally found someone who likes to work as late as you do, Ms. Santiago."

"Well, I guess you're right." Although frankly, she'd never had Patrick pegged as a workaholic before this.

"If it's going to be another one of those all-nighters, guess you don't want me to empty the wastebaskets in this room. I learned that rule the hard way."

"Yes, we lost the better part of a house one night in the garbage."

She noticed the puzzled look on Patrick's face. "The rough drafts, I mean."

The custodian bent down to pick up a piece of paper from the floor. "And I haven't thrown out anything in here without permission since. By the way, don't worry about your office. I already took care of the trash in there. Now it won't smell like Chinese food tomorrow morning."

"Curtis, I need to talk to you out in the hall for a minute."

He smiled as she followed him into the hallway and rifled through the garbage at the top of his trash cart until she found two pairs of chopsticks. "These were put in here by mistake."

"Whatever you say, Ms. Santiago."

ELEVEN

A month later, Jacki couldn't think of another man she'd rather strangle than Patrick Godwin. She had managed just fine with the project during his two weeks back in Maine, but now he was driving her slowly but surely crazy. Since he'd come back to Arizona, he'd issued at least a dozen change orders to the house without consulting her. They were minor enough in cost, but the paperwork they created was annoying. And inevitably, they delayed the project's finish date.

She noticed that Patrick's motorcycle was already at the jobsite. This surprised her, since it wasn't even six o'clock yet. Closing her car door, she casually walked toward the house, shielding her eyes from the glare of the early morning sun. He normally didn't visit the job site until closer to seven or eight, which she didn't mind because it gave her at least an hour or two to work there without him distracting her. And God help him, he was a major distraction. Today he was early. Something had to be up.

From her vantage point above the house, the site appeared to be crawling with worker ants. Smiling, she switched her favorite baseball hat for a hard hat, and headed toward the construction trailer. She could hear the framers pounding away and Mike's voice shouting at the mason. A nearby forklift kicked up dust from the desert floor.

As she reached the trailer, she stomped the desert dust off her boots, and stepped inside. The cool, dimly lit trailer was empty.

Thumbing through the change orders on the desk beside her, Jacki began to read a lengthy revision request for the windows on the back of the house. This change would mean a total rebuild for that part of the structure. At a cost of about thirty thousand dollars, it was nothing to sneeze at. The change was initiated by none other than Patrick Godwin. Apparently, he'd had second thoughts about the design of the rear elevation. He'd revised the arched palladian windows into rectangles with exposed pine lintels. Sure, the effect would be dazzling, but the added cost was astronomical, and the time delay most definitely unacceptable.

Tossing the paperwork aside, she took off her hard hat and rubbed her temples. Damn his quest for that medallion! Is this what he spent his time in Maine doing—thinking of ways to complicate this project and drive the construction manager mad? He didn't have a clue as to how much extra work this would mean for her and Mike. And the crew. At least Patrick had better not have a clue.

All he seemed to think he had to do was wave his magic pencil over a piece of paper, and his job was done. They had to make it work. He didn't. This was a nightmare. Since the house was nearly fully framed, the framers were scheduled on another job the next week, and wouldn't be available for two months at the least. There was no way she could execute these changes in seven days, but it sure wouldn't take that long to execute the architect.

Jerking open the center desk drawer, she dug through the contents until she found the bottle of antacids. Why was it that she practically ate these like candy when Patrick was on the jobsite? Popping two of them into her mouth, she chewed viciously.

Well, there was no way to avoid a confrontation. It was her job to manage the project, and she wasn't going to let her growing feelings for the architect get in the way of her duties.

Slamming the trailer door behind her, she trudged off toward the house with the certainty that her morning was ruined.

There he was, at the back of the house, bent over the blueprints, looking completely unstressed, oblivious to the mess that he'd made of her project budget and schedule. She wanted to whack him on the head with a two-by-four.

Just at that moment, he looked up and gave her a lopsided grin, making her heart thump double time.

Every day, Patrick looked better to her. Although considering how gorgeous he was to begin with, she wouldn't have believed any improvement was possible. Since his arrival in Arizona, he'd acquired a deep, rich tan.

Today, he was wearing a light blue polo shirt that made his eyes seem even bluer. The soft fabric of the shirt pulled across the expanse of his broad chest, emphasizing every single muscle. The jeans, which were now part of his standard garb, hugged his thighs and hips as though they had been designed especially for him.

He shouted a greeting over the construction noise. "Good morning, Jacki. Bet you're surprised to see me out here this early. Did you see those changes to the back of the house? Stroke of genius, huh?"

Walking over toward him, she rapped him on the hard hat with the rolled-up change orders in her hand. It wasn't a two-by-four, but it did the job.

"Hey, what'd you do that for?" He put his hand up to his head.

"That was for submitting that huge change order without at least going over it with me first." She hit him again. "That's for making a change that will overrun the project in both cost and time." She lifted her arm once more, but he stymied her by moving away.

Out of the corner of her eye she saw that some of the workers were starting to notice her fury. She held back her next shot. "Let's take this discussion into the trailer," she said, taking shallow breaths.

"Hey Pat, keep that hard hat on!" one of the men shouted.

Her heart pounded as they stepped inside, but she wasn't sure whether it was from the physical exertion or the fact that hitting him made her want to grab and kiss him. In fact, everything seemed to make her want to grab Patrick and kiss him. She had to be losing her mind.

"Are you trying to hurt me or something?"

"Well, if I was, I sure wouldn't be using a few sheets of paper on a hard hat. I guess I should have used that two-by-four after all."

Patrick sighed. It was going to be a long morning,

and an even longer day. There had to be an easier way to get Jacqueline Santiago on his side.

"Mia, can you get that? I'm in my robe. I'm not decent. Mia?" Then Jacki remembered it was Wednesday, the night Mia went with her buddies to the discount show at the movies to see the newest love story and catch up on the latest gossip. "Darn!"

The doorbell rang again. Jacki pressed the intercom button. "Who is it, and what do you want?" she asked irritably.

A deep, baritone voice at the other end answered. "Flowers for Ms. Santiago."

"Just a minute. Let go of my robe! Give me that slipper! I don't have time to play games. Someone's at the door."

Patrick frowned at the exchange he was hearing over the intercom. Who was Jacki playing games with?

The door swung open, and Bart jumped out with an orange synthetic fur Garfield slipper in his mouth.

Jacki leaped beside Bart, bent over, and tried to grab the slipper from his mouth. As she leaned over, her emerald green terry cloth robe gaped open, revealing her state of undress beneath it. A shapely thigh as well as the gentle softness of her feminine curves were clearly exposed. For the first time, Patrick saw her glorious hair unbound and flowing over her shoulders and down her back. Jacki straightened up. Face red from exertion, she held the slipper triumphantly in the air.

When she saw the delivery boy was none other than Patrick, she realized, much to her chagrin, that a lot of her was suddenly on display. She tried to close the gap at the top and the one at the bottom of her robe at the same time.

Patrick felt as if his eyes were popping out of his head. She looked incredibly desirable with her hair down like that.

"Uh, hi. I just happened to be out this way . . ." He patted Bart on the head. "Hi there, boy. I don't have any double pepperoni pizza for you today. Sorry."

Jacki wasn't fooled by Patrick's quick recovery and his casual comments to her dog. She had felt his penetrating look all the way through her, like a jolt of lightning. Jacki realized how much of her body he had seen. Somehow, although she was still embarrassed by his previous attention, she wished he would stop talking to Bart and look at her again. Now. The man made her mind turn to mush, she thought hopelessly.

Patrick handed her a large box.

"Belgian chocolates? Five pounds? All for me?"

"Unless you want to share them with Bart."

"Are you kidding?"

"I couldn't decide between candy and flowers . . ."

"Oh, this was definitely a better choice."

"So I brought you both." He picked up a long box that was propped up against the side of the house.

"No one has ever given me flowers. Not even—"

"Not even?" he prodded.

"Not even . . . oh, never mind. Come on inside. I'll make us some coffee and you can apologize."

"Don't you mean that you can apologize to me? After all, you're the one that hit me with those killer papers." He followed her through the quiet house into the kitchen.

"Apologize? In your dreams. You wouldn't have felt a baseball bat hitting you on the head under that hard hat."

"Well, you could have given me a really bad paper cut."

Men are such whiners, Jacki thought, opening the cabinet door and taking out a bag of gourmet Colombian coffee beans. The whir of the grinder echoed throughout the kitchen and reverberated in the silence.

"Would you mind filling this with water?" She handed him the glass carafe from the coffeemaker. Her hand trembled as she poured the ground coffee into the gold filter, spilling some onto the floor.

"In my dreams?" Patrick set the carafe on the tiled counter by Jacki. "You can't even begin to imagine what's in my dreams."

She poured the water from the carafe into the top of the coffeemaker and snapped the plastic lid closed. "Oh, I can imagine." She turned on the switch. "Have a seat. This should only take a few minutes."

"The coffee, or your apology?" He gave her a heart-stopping smile.

She sighed. "The coffee, of course."

He sat down on one of the bar stools across the counter from her. Still too edgy to sit, she reached over and opened the box of flowers. "Sterling roses! How beautiful!"

Carefully, she picked up one of the lavender

blooms and held it to her nose. The delicate scent was intoxicating.

"These will look perfect in my crystal vase." Leaving the kitchen, she went in search of it.

While Jacki was gone, Patrick took the opportunity to look around the room. It was colorful, cheerful, eclectic. Shining copper-bottomed pans hung from large metal hooks in the center of the kitchen over the butcher block work island. The oversized refrigerator was covered with snapshots of Jacki, Bart, and Mia.

He tried to hide his disappointment when Jacki returned to the kitchen fully dressed. Her delightfully revealing robe was a thing of the past. A rubber band confined her sensuous locks to a tight ponytail. She was wearing a pair of ragged cutoffs and an oversized T-shirt with a printed sketch of two skeletons in lounge chairs, and the words "It's A Dry Heat," above them. Her sneakers looked as though Bart had chewed on them, but she was still gorgeous.

Jacki finished arranging the roses in the vase and briskly brushed her hands on her cutoffs. "There."

The smell of the coffee began to fill the kitchen. She reached in an upper cabinet and took down two matched ceramic mugs.

After adding cream and sweetener to his mug—and stirring it herself—she handed it to him.

"We've worked together all of these weeks and I don't know much about you, except that you're probably one of the most responsible people I know." He began to stir his coffee vigorously, then thought better of it.

"How so?"

"For one thing, you took over the company when your father died and managed it like a pro. You finished raising Mia, although it looks like you're still raising Bart."

"You'd have done the same thing."

He shrugged. "There is one thing I'm curious about, though. How did you get to know Winnie Longmont?"

"Winnie and my grandmother went to the same convent school in New Mexico. Even after my grandmother got married and moved to Arizona, they kept in touch. I have pictures of both of them in pigtails and identical school uniforms." She pushed Bart away from the candy again. "How is it that you know Winnie?"

"She's my godmother. Frankly, she spoiled me rotten."

Their hands touched as they reached for a piece of chocolate at the same time. Not saying a word, and still touching her hand, Patrick stood and walked to Jacki's side of the counter. She began to rise from her barstool. They stood facing each other, neither one of them moving. Jacki's heart was pounding so loudly she was sure Patrick could hear it. Every muscle in her body tensed.

"Patrick," she whispered. She threw her arms around his neck and pressed her body against his.

His eyes opened wide with surprise as her moist, inviting lips found his. As if surrendering, Patrick closed his eyes, and his mouth welcomed hers. He encircled her body with a strong embrace. Jacki tingled with desire, until a familiar voice shattered the air.

"Jacki, I'm home! Can you believe it? The film broke right in the middle of the big love scene." Mia stopped short at the sight of the couple's sensual embrace. "But I guess I didn't have to leave the house to see one . . ."

Patrick backed away from Jacki, the color of their faces a study in red.

As Mia covered her mouth and started giggling, Patrick whispered to Jacki, "Why is it we always seem to draw a crowd?"

Long after Patrick left her house that evening, Jacki sat in her bedroom at the rolltop desk that had belonged to her great-grandmother.

Mia popped into the room, not bothering to stop before she started speaking. "You've been in here a long time. Are you okay?"

"I think so . . . I'm not sure."

"That was some kiss I saw."

"Yeah, that was some kiss," Jacki agreed.

"Is that what you're thinking about?"

"No," she lied.

"Really? If Patrick had kissed me like that, I'd still be thinking about it."

"It isn't so much the kiss as the—"

"As the what? The body meld you guys were doing?"

"That's only part of what I'm thinking about."

"So what else is there to think about?"

"For starters, how I shouldn't be mixing business and pleasure. After all, Patrick is a client."

"No, Winnie's the client. He just works for her."

"Same difference. Besides, what if we do get a personal relationship started, and he turns out to be like Roc or Evan?"

"Patrick isn't Roc. And he sure isn't Evan. Don't start comparing them, because there's just no comparison."

"I feel so confused."

"That's because you're trying to use your head to figure out a matter of the heart. You have to be honest about what's in the old *corazón.*" Mia thumped her chest as she looked at the clock. "Gotta run. There's a movie on the Romance Channel I haven't seen yet."

"That has to be a first. *Buenas noches, prima.*"

"*Hasta mañana.*" Mia closed the door behind her as she left the room.

Jacki reached up and turned on the small Tiffany lamp that sat on the top of the desk. Pulling the center drawer open, she took out one of the chopsticks she'd saved from the night she'd spent working with Patrick, and tapped it absentmindedly on the desk. Kind of a funny thing to keep, she mused, but that Chinese dinner had been their first dinner date.

It was easier for her to stay calm and relaxed in her bedroom, surrounded by the things she loved, than just about anywhere else she could think of. She looked at the bed that had been in her family for generations. A colorful quilt her aunt had designed especially for her covered it. The walls were adorned with family portraits, a woven eye of God—*ojo de Dios*—which Mia had made in grade school, and a framed painting of Our Lady of Guadalupe with a sconce on either side. In this serene atmosphere, she would try to sort out her thoughts. Jacki wasn't sure what her final decision would be, but now she knew how to go about making it.

Mia was right. She had to be honest about what was in her heart. She had to remember that not everyone was like Evan. Not everyone was like Roc. She had to learn to trust again. But could she?

Whenever Jacki faced a tough decision at work, she made a detailed list of all of the pros and cons of the situation. It might help to approach the Patrick dilemma just as logically.

Jacki took the fountain pen her uncle had given her for her graduation from the desk drawer. She drew a line down the center of a piece of crisp, white stationery and titled the first column *Good Things About Patrick* in bold architectural lettering. She took the chopstick and rolled it slowly across the desk while she thought.

Number One. Patrick is extremely handsome, she wrote. Big deal—so was Roc. But she wasn't alone in her thoughts about Patrick. All the women she knew thought he was the best-looking man they'd ever seen in their life. Maybe she was being too superficial, she chided herself.

Jacki wrote again. *Number Two. Patrick is loyal.* He was spending all of this time in Arizona out of loyalty to Winnie and her project. She heard Bart whining at the door, and as she opened it, he bounded into the room. Jacki laughed. Bart was loyal, too.

She returned to the desk. *Number Three. Patrick is generous.* When the whole crew had to work late, he'd bought pizza for everyone. And he was always bringing in treats for the staff. Try as she might, Jacki couldn't contradict that.

Number Four. Patrick has a sense of humor. Well, more so around Mia.

He sounds like a Boy Scout, Jacki thought wryly, switching gears.

Bad Things About Patrick, she titled over the second column. *Number One. Patrick is extremely handsome.* Everywhere he went, women threw themselves at him. It was unnerving.

Number Two. Patrick flirts with everyone. Okay, it was just with women, and it didn't seem to matter what size, shape, or age they were. To be honest, it seemed to her that they always flirted with him first. And it never got beyond the flirting stage.

Number Three. Patrick is stubborn. It was a good thing she was stubborn, too, or they would never get anything done right.

Number Four. Patrick won't listen. He still refused to admit some of his ideas were unworkable. She had to remind him about this a lot.

Jacki put down the pen. This wasn't working. Love didn't lend itself to a balance sheet. There was absolutely no logic to her feelings for Patrick.

She forced herself to look at the bottom line. How did she truly feel about him? He made her feel like no one else ever had. Even Evan. Especially Evan.

Every fiber in her body was aware of Patrick. As much effort as she'd put into trying to keep him at a distance, she had failed miserably. In the midst of all of this confusion, there was one undeniable fact— she, Jacqueline Milagra Santiago, the woman who had officially sworn off men for the indefinite future, was head over heels, hopelessly, helplessly, and irrevocably in love.

TWELVE

A month later, Patrick sat at his desk back at his office in Maine. He'd left his window open. Leaning out of it, he took a deep breath of the cool morning air. Soon, the days would be colder, and the leaves of the huge oak and maple trees surrounding the building would trade their summer green for their autumnal reds and golds. He knew he should have been thinking about the local projects they were working on, but somehow, all of his thoughts kept returning to Jacki. She sure was something. Full of drive. Totally committed to the project. And the way she handled the work crews—he could certainly use her here in Maine just about now.

"Thinking about throwing yourself out of the window already?" Derek, his assistant, came through the door with the secretary, Ruth. "I know I would be."

Patrick pulled his head back inside and looked at the duo. "Problems?"

"Take a look at this, boss." Ruth, a skinny woman with thick gray hair, held out a sheet of paper. "The first column is what we owe our consultants. The second one is what we've been paid to date."

"Yeah, if it wasn't for the Longmont project, we'd all be out on the streets," Derek added.

Patrick took the paper from his secretary and looked at the figures. It wasn't as bad as Derek, an eternal pessimist, had indicated. "I'll just cover this out of my personal account until the payments start coming in again. Don't worry. This is just a temporary lull."

"But instead of spending all of your time in Arizona, you need to be going out and drumming up some more business." Derek ran his hand through his sandy hair. "I've tried, but I'm just not as good at that sort of thing as you are."

"Derek has tried hard. He's done at least five presentations this month alone. It's just that he doesn't have your . . . charisma."

"Gee, thanks a lot, Ruth," Derek griped.

She smiled apologetically at him.

"Remember, Ruth, we hired Derek for his analytical skills, not his personality," Patrick added, setting the paper on his desk.

"Well, that makes me feel a lot better."

"I'll file this where it belongs." Ruth picked the paper back up. "Seriously, boss, prospective clients want to have the principal architect do the dog and pony show. You send in an underling, and bang— they immediately get the feeling that you don't care enough about getting their business. Without the right players, you lose the game before it's even started."

"Ruth's right. That's why we made this for you." Derek held out a binder.

Opening it up, Patrick knew exactly why they'd

joined forces to present this document to him. "Why, this seems to be a description of upcoming government projects here in Maine." He groaned inwardly. He'd rather not have to make decisions like this right now.

Relentlessly, Ruth reached over and flipped through the pages. "Here's a convention center. A public safety building. Several fire stations. And a library. You've always wanted to do a library."

"Think about it, Patrick. These projects could keep us busy for the next three or four years." Derek shoved his hands in his pockets, crossed the room, and looked out the window.

"I know why you're so worried. Now that you have a new baby and all . . ." Patrick put his hand on Derek's shoulder. "It's going to be all right. Even if we have to relocate to Phoenix, there's work. Lots of it."

Ruth said, "Even if we did get awarded these government contracts, money wouldn't start coming in for at least the next six months. You both know how slow the government is when it comes to paying people. We need private sector projects. And we need them now. Those two local projects that we do have are going to be wrapped up in the next few weeks." She joined them at the window.

Patrick walked over to his desk and flipped through his calendar. "In the meantime, Ruth, have you heard anything more from your brother-in-law about those remodeling projects for his warehouses?"

"He says that he needs some of the renovations done right away."

"That should keep us solvent, at least through the

winter. I'll give him a call this morning." Patrick gave his coworkers a reassuring smile. "And don't forget, when we win the Mitchell Burrell Medallion of Excellence, clients will be beating down the door for our architectural services."

"If we win it."

"There's no 'if' here, Derek. We will win it. We have to win it."

The phone rang, interrupting their conversation. "I've got it," Patrick told Ruth as she reached for it.

The voice he'd been longing to hear was on the other end. "Hi, Jacki. I've missed you."

Giving Ruth and Derek a long, meaningful, get-lost look, he waited until they'd left the room and closed the door to his office behind them before he continued the conversation.

"Patrick, you've been gone for two weeks now, and you still haven't told me when you're coming back. Can you make it here for the Labor Day weekend?"

"You miss me?" Patrick prompted, sitting on the edge of his desk.

"Well, Mia misses you. And Mike misses you. But Bart really misses you."

"Bart misses my double pepperoni pizza." He reached up and loosened his tie. "But do you miss me?"

"Maybe just a little."

"That's good to hear." He took a deep breath. "Look, Jacki, I'm afraid I won't be back in Phoenix by Labor Day. I have to wrap up a few things here, so it's going to be at least two or three more weeks before I make it back to Arizona."

"Well, I won't say I'm not disappointed, but I

know how time consuming the wrap-up on projects can be. Just don't be gone too long. You won't believe everything that's been finished on the house."

Patrick began doodling on the edge of his calendar. "Tell me more." He just wanted to hear her voice. When she got all excited about something, her voice got deliciously husky, and it made his imagination run wild.

"The framers have finally finished the openings for those windows you wanted. And the electricians and plumbers have already begun their work. And we're actually ahead of schedule and on budget. Knock on wood."

"See, it didn't take as long as you thought it would."

"Yeah, but just don't make any more changes. My heart can't take it."

"Well, when I get back, we'll see how much that heart of yours can take." He drew a heart on his calendar.

"Promise?" Her voice sounded even lower. Huskier.

"You can count on it." He smiled as he hung up the phone.

Three weeks later, Jacki took Patrick straight from the airport to the Longmont job site. "The grand tour begins here," she announced, taking him inside the house. "So, what do you think of the progress?"

She had been right, he thought. He couldn't believe everything she had accomplished. "This is impressive."

Throwing her arms out wide, she twirled around the magnificent, albeit empty, front hall. "My goodness, you could fit three or four houses in this room alone," she exaggerated blithely. "This is going to be the best house in the whole world!"

He watched as she flew around the space, then laughingly captured her. As he swept her into his arms, his playful demeanor took on a more serious tone. "Jacki, did I ever tell you that—"

There was a loud crackle as the lights went out. The humming of the generator was replaced by a low, howling sound. The windows began to reverberate as the desert winds gathered their forces.

"What in the world was that?" he asked with surprise.

"Just a monsoon, although this is really late in the season to get one." Her nonchalant tone belied the intensity of the emotions coursing through her body.

A flash of lightning broke the darkness and illuminated her face for an instant. Patrick tightened his embrace just as an earsplitting clap of thunder shook the room. He threaded his fingers through her hair, pulling her even closer. His lips found hers in the darkness.

Her body melted against his. He was astonished at how well they fit together.

His tongue slowly outlined her lips. She eagerly parted her mouth and languorously teased his tongue with hers. Patrick emitted a low groan. He had never wanted anyone with the intensity he wanted this jet-haired beauty. Their kiss became deeper.

He felt her soft hands slip under his shirt, lightly

caressing his back. A little voice inside Patrick cautioned him to stop while he could. Judging from the way things were going, he wouldn't be able to much longer.

He was through being patient. He wanted her so much he was in physical pain. After all, he had been a virtual saint these last few months, hadn't he? Instincts as old as the first man dominated his thoughts, his actions, his deeds. He vowed he was going to make her his. Tonight.

The violence of the sudden storm outside made them bolder, more daring.

The pressure of Patrick's kiss forced Jacki to back up against a wall for support. He cupped her face with his hands and stroked her cheeks as he gently kissed her face. He untied the leather thong at the end of her braid, and combed through the plait with his fingers, releasing the thick, fragrant mass of her hair.

The feel of Patrick, the unique smell of Patrick— they were driving her to the brink. She began to unbutton his shirt. Jacki pulled it open with both hands, freeing his chest for her own exploration. Her lips left a trail of kisses from his neck down to his collarbone across to his shoulder.

The lights came on as abruptly as they had gone off.

"Damn!" Patrick uttered the curse with great feeling.

The sudden brightness hurt their eyes. Jacki blinked her eyes, her passionate mood evaporating with the darkness. Her common sense, which had served her so long and so well, began to return. She reminded herself that he was leaving for good in a few months, and there was no reason she should be getting involved with him.

Ruefully, she pulled his shirt together and rebuttoned it with shaking fingers. She patted him on the chest. "That was close," she commented in a tremulous voice.

He pulled her tight and sighed. "Yes, it was," he agreed. "You'd better take me home now."

She nodded silently, more saddened than relieved that their unexpected amorous interlude had ended. She had kept her promise to herself. She should be feeling better. Right?

Wrong. The drive home seemed interminable, and filled with long and uncomfortable periods of silence. Neither of them seemed to know what to say. Jacki stared straight out the windshield of the Cherokee, but the damage which the fierce summer storm had wrought didn't register with her. She gazed right through the broken tree branches that littered the ground and the dangling road signs as though they were invisible.

Suddenly, the traffic ahead of her stopped. Slamming on the brakes, Jacki snapped out of her trance and broke the silence. "I'm sorry, Patrick. I should have been paying more attention. We shouldn't have come this way, because the road up ahead floods every time there's even a light shower. We'll have to wait until the other cars have had a chance to turn around out of this mess before we can go anywhere."

Patrick noticed the other motorists climbing out of their cars to look around. A raging river now ran, where moments before there had been only a dust-filled ravine. Curious, he got out, leaving her sitting alone in the car. Jacki was thankful for the ensuing moment of solitude.

She needed some time to think. What would have happened if the lights in the house hadn't come on when they did? Was she ready for that level of intimacy with Patrick? What about her promise to herself not to make love with anyone unless there was a long-term commitment? Was she wrong in assuming commitment would automatically follow their lovemaking? What would happen when Patrick went back to Maine? And he *was* returning to Maine—she was sure of it.

Jacki rested her arm on the frame of the opened car window, ignoring the drops of moisture that still clung to it. She placed her chin on her forearm and looked out at nothing in particular, considering the possibility of Patrick making love with her. They had been frighteningly close. Excitedly close . . . Jacki was so wrapped up in her thoughts she didn't hear Patrick as he came up to her side of the car.

Patrick leaned down until he could put his head through the window. "I'm sorry," he whispered.

"About what? Starting—or stopping?" Jacki wondered.

"I don't know," Patrick responded honestly. "Both. Neither. All I know is it feels so damn good to hold you in my arms."

Jacki reached out of the car and took his hand. She brought it to her lips and softly brushed his knuckles with a kiss. "And all I know is it feels so damn good to have you hold me in your arms. I'm sorry, too."

"For what?"

"For stopping when the lights came on," she admitted.

Patrick smiled at her. "Well, blackouts can be arranged," he said softly.

"When?" she asked, almost without thinking.

"When you least expect it . . ."

THIRTEEN

This had to have been the fiftieth outfit she'd put on for her first date with Patrick. They had gone out before . . . several times. But this was a real, honest-to-goodness I'm-calling-you-several-days-in-advance-and-we'll-go-somewhere-special-and-dance sort of date.

And her self-appointed fashion advisor Mia, who sat on Jacki's bed next to a drowsy Bart, wasn't being much help. "I tell you, Jacki, you need to show more leg. You've got a great set of legs, and you keep hiding them with those blue jeans."

"I work at a construction site, *prima,* not on a designer's runway. And besides, the last thing those guys need to see is my legs." She shimmied out of a red sequinned miniskirt that belonged to Mia. "Where did you put that green dress you wore when you went to that awards banquet with Randy?"

"Sheath." Mia shook out the red miniskirt and put it back on the hanger. "It's an emerald sheath."

"Okay. What did you do with the emerald sheath you wore when you went to that awards banquet with Randy?"

"I have it in my closet. But I don't think it will fit you."

"We're both tall."

"That's true, but one of us has more on top than the other."

"Not that much more." Glancing down at her chest, Jacki did a quick comparison.

"I think you're wrong, cuz," Mia contradicted, "but I'll go get the dress anyway."

"You mean the sheath," Jacki corrected with a smile. After her cousin left, she turned sideways, looked in the mirror, and adjusted her bra strap. "And I'm not that much bigger."

"You are so."

Jacki jumped away from the mirror. "Hand over the dress. And no comments." Stepping into the gown, she pulled the chiffon-like fabric up over her hips. "Will you please zip me up, Mia?"

"Here goes. Suck it in." The zipper glided up easily until the middle of her back. "Well, so much for this outfit. The zipper won't go any further."

"It has to. Try harder," Jacki insisted, using both hands to smoosh her bosom flatter.

"I don't want to break the zipper and ruin my dress," Mia objected.

"Just zip the dress." Jacki pressed down harder and stood perfectly still.

"Mission accomplished. Can you still move your arms?"

"Don't be silly."

As Jacki put her hands at her sides, all of the flesh she'd compressed burst forward, making a statement of its own over the edge of the scoop neck.

"Wow. I had no idea . . ." Mia's tone was almost reverent. "You know, maybe your legs are your second best feature."

"I can't wear this thing. I'm falling out of it."

"Before you make me unzip it, take a look in the mirror."

Jacki stood in front of the mirror and turned from side to side. "Great look for a call girl. Or a model for a minimizer bra."

Mia looked at her carefully. "You look more like a maximizer model."

"Then unzip me."

"I'm not sure I can. Besides, that color is great on you. It matches your eyes. And look, the scarf that goes with it covers most of what you're exposing."

Taking the scarf from Mia, Jacki wrapped it once around her neck and draped it artfully over her bust-line. "Not bad."

"Oh-oh." Mia pointed to the dress.

"What's wrong?"

"I can see your panty line."

"Where?" Smoothing the dress, front and back, Jacki couldn't feel anything amiss.

"Everywhere your panties are. Take a look."

Twisting to see what her cousin was talking about, she noticed right away that Mia's observation was on target. "It is pretty obvious, isn't it?"

"Yes, it is, but I have the perfect solution. Wait right here."

One minute later, Mia rushed back with a familiar erotically decorated box.

"Oh no. Not that leopard print thong."

"Want to wear the dress? Wear the thong. Or noth-ing."

"Hand me the damned thing."

Just as Jacki wiggled out of her underwear and replaced it with the thong, the doorbell rang. Bart, suddenly alert, sprang from the bed to greet their visitor. "Mia, can you get that? I still have to put on my jewelry and find my shoes. Tell Patrick I'll be a couple more minutes."

Opening her jewelry box, she'd just pulled out her diamond stud earrings when she heard Mia and Bart greet Patrick.

"Zowie kapowie," Mia squealed. "Look at you! My gosh, you're even cuter than Antonio Banderas! Jacki! Come and look at Patrick! He's awesome—all decked out in a tuxedo and everything!"

"In a minute. I'll be right there." Mia was always exaggerating. No one could possibly be as handsome as Antonio.

Fastening her bracelet, Jacki stepped into the foyer. One glance at Patrick, and she froze in her tracks. Darned if Mia wasn't right. He did look better than Antonio.

Patrick still stood at the front door. "Do you ladies mind if I come in? It's getting a little chilly out here." He rubbed his hands together.

"Mia, don't just stand there. Let the man in." Mia had to do it. She wasn't able to get her feet to move yet.

As Patrick stepped into the room and his eyes adjusted to the light, he caught sight of a vision in green. Jacki's ebony hair was swept up off her shoulders, and a few soft tendrils framed her face. He held out his hand. "You look beautiful. Your eyes have never looked greener or more lovely."

Mia punched him on the arm. "You don't look so bad yourself, Patrick."

Jacki took his hand. "Don't you have something you need to do, Mia?" she asked, her gaze never straying from him.

Mia sighed. "You guys look as good together as Barbie and Ken."

"And now would be a good time for you and Bart to go in and play with them."

"Oh, I get it. You two want to be alone." Taking the dog by the collar, Mia headed toward the back of the house.

Patrick could only nod his assent. A breeze coming through the still open door lifted the scarf around Jacki's neck and he was treated to a view of everything nature had endowed her with. He was in love, more so than ever. The night to come held promises beyond his imagination. He just knew it. He hadn't been turned on this much just by looking at a woman since the first episode of *Baywatch*. But Jacki made those dumb beach bunnies look positively anorexic.

He cleared his throat. "Are you ready to go?"

"I need to get my purse first."

As she turned to go, his mouth popped open. The slit in the back of the dress came clear up to her other assets. Maybe when she got back she'd drop the purse and have to bend over. He could always hope.

Unfortunately, she returned with her beaded purse clutched securely in one hand and her dress coat in the other.

Well, maybe she'd drop it later.

He helped her into her coat. "Oh, I almost forgot

the most important thing." Reaching into his vest pocket, he pulled out the black velvet sleep mask he'd bought earlier in the day. "Do you care if I blindfold you until we get to where we're going? I want it to be a surprise."

Actually, the blindfold was more of a shock than a surprise to her, but Jacki trusted him, so she decided to play along. "Promise you'll take it off as soon as we get to wherever we're going?"

Putting his hand over his heart, he swore solemnly, "I promise."

She held the plush mask to her face while he tied the satiny ribbons in the back, taking great care not to disturb her meticulously styled hair. "Now what?" she asked.

"Take my arm, and I'll escort you to the car."

Tucking her arm in his, they made their way slowly down the brick path, her high heels tapping on the uneven surface.

"You have a car?"

"I rented one for the evening."

They stopped. She heard a car door open. Patrick put his hand on her shoulder and guided her into the vehicle. "Watch your head." Gently, he buckled her seatbelt.

When he closed the door, she shifted in the seat, straightening her dress as best she could. She hoped she wasn't exposing any more flesh than she did standing up.

She felt the movement of the car as he climbed into the driver's seat, and then heard the familiar click of a seatbelt being fastened.

"Before we start, I have something to give you. First, a kiss."

She puckered up and waited. There was the sound of paper rustling. Lips still in kiss formation, she tilted up her head.

"Open your mouth," he whispered. "This isn't tofu."

So he was getting down to business right away. She could deal with that. She opened her mouth slightly, expecting a deep kiss of the French variety.

But instead of Patrick kissing her, he gave her a piece of chocolate. "Your first kiss of the evening. Are you ready?"

Nodding, she smiled as the chocolate slowly melted in her mouth. His gesture, corny but touching, reinforced her trust in him.

"Now hold out your hand."

What was he doing now? Expecting a handful of kisses, she was rewarded instead with what felt like a single rose. She raised it to her face and inhaled. That's what it was, all right. A gloriously scented rose. "It smells heavenly. It must be very beautiful."

"It's not as beautiful as you are. But nothing could be."

She stroked the fragrant petals with her hand. "It feels so soft."

There was another click followed by music. It sounded as though the entire New York Philharmonic was in the backseat of the car playing love songs just for the two of them.

If Patrick Godwin was intent on seduction, he was certainly on the right track.

* * *

Jacki could scarcely contain her excitement as the car came to a final stop. Just to confuse her, Patrick had taken an intricate route of turns and stops and more turns. She had no idea where they were.

The cold November air hit her as the car door opened.

He helped her out. "Take my arm. We're almost there."

Gravel crunched under their feet for a few yards, then Patrick warned, "Careful. There are three steps up."

She heard him unlock a door, and he assisted her in to wherever they were with a gentle pressure on the small of her back.

"Can I look yet?" Jacki was getting impatient.

"No. Just stand right there, and don't move an inch."

"I think you're enjoying telling me what to do a little too much."

She took a small step to the side and bumped into a wall.

"I told you not to budge." She could hear Patrick chuckling as he guided her carefully up a long flight of stairs. She smelled the delicious fragrance of expensive perfumed candles. Either he had brought her to a church—or a candlelit boudoir. She hoped for the latter.

"Can I look yet?"

As she reached up to remove the mask, she felt his hand nudging it back down, and he brought her into an unseen room. "Not yet. Be patient. It'll just be a couple of more minutes, and I promise you right now that it will be worth every second."

A Celtic melody filled the room, its sensuous rhythm beginning to build momentum. Jacki began to sway back and forth. The music relaxed her like a fine wine.

"Here, let me take your coat." How did he get behind her without making a sound?

"And the blindfold?"

"Comes off now." Untying the strings, he tossed it aside.

She blinked a couple of times. "We're at Winnie's house! In the master suite!"

"I think of it as the mistress suite," Patrick teased.

Dozens of scented candles lined the room, their fragrance bewitching her. Shadows flickered and seemed to dance on the walls to the giddy tempo of the music. The beguiling melody played on, a portent of temptations yet to come. "May I have this dance?" He held out his hand in invitation.

"I thought you'd never ask." She stepped forward and he swept her into his arms.

Their bodies merged together as they danced what was in their hearts, their steps slow and deliberate. Their gazes locked. "You're so beautiful," he murmured. "So very beautiful."

She rested her head on his shoulder, and for the first time in a long time, felt truly beautiful.

They might have glided together for five minutes or fifty. Time had no significance for Jacki, lost in the magic Patrick had created.

He kissed the side of her neck, sending tremors to the very tips of her fingers and toes. She lifted her mouth to his and, still moving to the pulse of the seductive strains, they shared a kiss as delicate as gossamer. His lips brushed her forehead, her cheek, her chin . . .

As the music quickened, Jacki opened her eyes. Putting her hand flat on his chest, she pushed him away from her, her body still swaying to the wild melody. Enticingly, inch by inch, she slipped the chiffon scarf from her shoulders, her hips punctuating every beat, every nuance, of the music.

She noticed that his entire attention seemed to be riveted on the swell of her bosom, and began to twirl and spin with an intricate footwork that she made up as she went along. Teasing. Tantalizing. Tempting. And at this very moment, Patrick looked as though he were totally and completely mesmerized, giving her a sense of power she'd never experienced before. As far as she was concerned, no world existed outside of this room. He was the only man, and she the only woman.

When the song ended, she paused, flushed and out of breath. His eyes burned into hers, his desire matching hers. He shrugged out of his jacket and stepped forward. She captured him with her diaphanous scarf, pulling him toward her, making unspoken promises with each gentle tug of the fabric. He looked dazed. She liked it.

The minute they touched, Jacki's body rebelled against the constraints of her clothing. She wanted only to be skin to skin with this man, and she could tell Patrick wanted her, too, as soon as his lips crushed down against hers. He tasted mysterious. He tasted familiar. And she knew without a doubt that she would die if his lips left hers for even a second. Her hands tore at his clothes, a button from his shirt falling unheeded to the carpet, followed by another. And another.

His movements seemed as urgent, as eager as hers. She felt his long, artistic fingers search frantically for the zipper. Finding the stubborn fastener, he yanked on it impatiently, swearing under his breath as he tore it in his frustration.

She helped him push the tight sheath dress over her hips. As his fingers slid down her thighs, she quivered in anticipation. Moaning, she shoved his shirt open, and began her own exploration of his chest, tracing his nipples with her tongue, smiling to herself as he quivered, too. She could taste the salt from the fine sheen of perspiration that was beginning to appear on his skin. Impatiently, she pushed his shirt off the rest of the way. As she outlined the contours of his chest with her fingertips, he whispered endearments against her hair.

With each sensuous touch, each fiery stroke, her need for him magnified. Impatiently, she grasped his belt.

Putting his hand over hers, he stepped back, out of reach. "Not yet," he commanded gruffly. "I want to look at you."

Well, she wanted to look at him, too.

The desire in Patrick's voice made Jacki's knees weaken and her pulse quicken. Reluctantly, she stepped away from him, watching as his eyes began a leisurely tour of her body. His obvious enjoyment made her feel courageous, even brazen. Smiling seductively, Jacki loosened her hair and shook it free. She reached behind her and unfastened her bra, slowly discarding it on top of her other clothes.

She saw him swallow as she exposed her breasts. His gaze didn't shift until she began to do a slow shimmy out of the leopard-print thong panties. Judging from the expression on his face, her decision to wear it had been a good one.

"Never in my wildest dreams . . ." he rasped.

"Oh, this isn't a dream," she promised, as she finished wiggling out of the thong, tossing it to one side.

He was out of the rest of his clothes in a heartbeat, and the last of them had no sooner hit the floor when Jacki and Patrick descended together onto the rumpled garments. Nothing besides Patrick mattered, not even the broken zipper that was poking at her from the dress she lay on. All rational thought disappeared as his insistent lips and inventive hands began a feverish search of her body. Jacki arched against Patrick, urging him on with soft whispers and murmured words of love.

She threaded her fingers through his hair and pulled his mouth to hers. He kissed her with a fierce hunger as she caressed the length of his back, her breasts crushed against the hardness of his chest.

As her need grew stronger, mere kisses and touches weren't enough. It was time. The need to be joined with this man consumed her. Jacki felt the roughness of the carpet on her hip as she rolled on top of him. She heard Patrick gasp as she lowered her body over his. He pulled her onto his chest, branding her with rough kisses, and making love to her with a passion that burned far brighter than the hundred flames of the candles that lined the room.

FOURTEEN

"Okay, that's it. That's the last time I ever lend you one of my outfits. Ever." Mia held up what was left of the emerald green sheath and shook it in her cousin's face. "Look at this! The zipper is completely disintegrated. How did the hem get ripped out? And see all these snags?" Dropping the battered sheath, she picked up the scarf and held it up to the light. "What's this on my scarf? Lipstick? How did you get lipstick on my scarf? The whole outfit is totally ruined."

"What time is it?" Rubbing her eyes, Jacki propped herself on her elbow and squinted at Mia from the warmth of her bed.

"Time for you to get out of that bed and buy me a new dress to replace this one."

"I'm sorry, *prima*. I guess we just got a little . . . carried away." Jacki rolled to her side and groaned. "Ow. That hurts," she complained, rolling back over and massaging a place on the side of her hip.

"What's wrong?" Pushing Jacki's nightshirt aside, Mia peered at the abrasion. "Carpet burn?" She looked her cousin straight in the face. "Okay. Was it like the song—was it in his kiss? You have to tell me everything. You owe me."

"What makes you think it's carpet burn?" Jacki pulled herself out of bed and realized she was deliciously sore all over. Whatever had made her think that she could pretend to be an acrobat, gypsy dancer, and legendary temptress all in one, and not pay for it later? Her body was never meant to be that flexible. She wondered if Patrick was feeling any pain today. They were too old to be rolling around on a hard floor like a couple of teenagers. But boy, once he started kissing her . . .

"Oh, I know it's carpet burn, all right. Patrick told me where you were going before he left. I know for a fact that there's no furniture at Winnie's yet. And my dress wouldn't have been demolished if you guys had stuck to dancing."

Jacki threw on her robe. "You don't know what kind of dancing we did. Besides, I refuse to discuss this with you. I'll buy you a new dress, but some things are private."

"Just don't do things like that in my clothes any more," Mia called after her as she headed for the shower.

Even the hair on the back of his hand was sore, Patrick realized as he reached over to answer his wake-up call. He was remembering muscles he didn't know he had. He wondered if Jacki was hurting as much as he was. The woman sure had stamina. And imagination.

He glanced over at his tuxedo. Wrinkled and torn

in several places, it was in bad shape. His shirt, thrown on the floor by his bed, was even worse. He leaned over and picked it up. Where in the world were all the buttons? And how had he gotten candle wax on the sleeves? He wasn't even sure which one of them was wearing the shirt when it happened. They could have burned the house down. And they wouldn't have known it. He grinned.

Last night had been educational, though. He'd picked up some interesting new Spanish words and phrases.

Stretching his arms over his head, he winced. There was another muscle complaining about his adventures. He remembered the sounds she'd made at the height of her passion, the silken feel of her hair falling through his fingers, the look in her eyes as she danced for him. And what a dance it had been.

Unfortunately, he couldn't even take the day off to recuperate. Groaning, he got out of the hotel bed. It was moving day. Time to get all of Winnie's furniture and treasures into her new house.

Not one, but a caravan of semis brought the furniture for Winnie's house. And all the movers wanted to get in the house at once. By the time Patrick got there, Jacki stood like a traffic cop at the front door directing the movers toward the east or west wing to either Randy or Mia, both of whom had a detailed floor plan for their assigned area.

"Oh good, you're here. I need you . . ."

"I know, I feel the same way." He kissed her on the nose.

"Patrick. Stop it. People can see us." She batted him away with her hands, but her smile was radiant. "I need you to monitor the central area of the house. Here's your floor plan." He knew what to do. They'd planned this for weeks, creating meticulous layouts for every piece of Winnie's furniture.

He squeezed her hand and went off to his station in the living room. This move should go like clockwork. With any luck, the movers would be gone in a couple of hours, and the decorators they'd hired to unpack and arrange all Winnie's belongings would come in. Figuring out where to put all the artwork, bibelots and other personal items would be a painstaking job.

An hour later, Jacki knew the move wasn't going smoothly. And it had to be all Patrick's fault. Just as she thought all the furniture had been moved in, several pieces were making their way back out.

"Excuse me." Jacki tapped one of the movers on the shoulder. "What are you doing with this sofa? Didn't the man with the floor plan show you where it goes?" Before she got an answer, she had to move quickly out of the way of three other movers hoisting the baby grand piano from inside the house to the driveway.

She had an idea what was going on. Mr. Change Order himself couldn't let anything be. He always had a better idea. Even if it wasn't. She marched to the living room. "Patrick Godwin, what's going on here?"

"What do you need, honey?" He looked up from

the floor plan he was sketching on. The paper was covered with little black arrows and squiggles.

"Don't 'honey' me. I know what you're doing. You're changing things at the last minute again."

"But it'll be better if we—"

"You and I worked on these layouts for hours. Together. In agreement."

"It's just a small change. Look what I found." He held out two small white buttons. They were from his tuxedo shirt, torn off the night before in their haste to make love.

She smiled, almost against her will.

Taking her into his arms, he kissed her, and just like the last time, she didn't want it to end. Mia was right. It was in his kiss. He loved her.

And she had to ask. "Patrick, we have to talk. Now. Are you staying, or are you going?"

He stroked her back. "How can I leave you? No one has ever meant this much to me. I love you, Jacki."

"Okay. You love her." A mover wedged his way between them. "Now where do you want this piano?"

"Right here." Patrick took the layout from Jacki and handed it to the mover. "Just like the plan says."

Winnie's house was finally complete. Standing in the spacious living room, Jacki looked around her in satisfaction. Every last problem, flaw, and omission cited on the to-do list had been corrected. Every mar, scrape, and scratch had been meticulously painted over. The windows and mirrors sparkled in the early morning sunshine. The hand-waxed wooden floors gleamed. Every last piece of Winnie's furniture—and there was plenty of it—had been arranged just so, and polished.

The odor of paint and the new carpet smell was still there, although the freshly cut flowers in every room of the house gave off a faint but distinctive fragrance of their own. These and other delicious scents teased Jacki's nostrils. Lemon oil. Sandalwood. Cinnamon potpourri.

The house was ready at last. A customized mat, woven with the images of Winnie's three cats, lay in front of the door, bidding welcome to all who entered. Winnie's knickknacks, which included an extensive collection of teapots, were arranged artfully throughout the house. Jacki took one down from the top of a curio cabinet and traced the outline of hand-painted violets on the fragile porcelain with her finger. Dozens of candles of assorted shapes and sizes sat in antique brass and cut crystal holders, gracing all six fireplace mantels.

Each room had its own built-in shelves which held hundreds of books on every subject imaginable. Jacki laughed out loud as she noticed the title of one of the volumes, *The Simple Life*. That one must have been strictly for show.

Never in a million years would Jacki have thought that the mixture of Winnie's eclectic furnishings and decor would have meshed so well with the starkness of the house's Macedonian/Egyptian architectural lines. But Patrick's offbeat genius and his outstanding talent had made them work. She had to take some of the credit, too. She'd had plenty of ideas of her own, and once Patrick actually began to trust her intuition, he'd incorporated those concepts into the overall design.

Winnie's three cats—whimsically named Peanut, Butter, and Jelly—had been brought back from her girlfriend's and nonchalantly roamed the new house in search of some special spots to take their early morning naps. The only thing missing from the house was Winnie Longmont herself, and Patrick was en route to the airport to get her, at that very minute.

Jacki had spent the whole night making sure every detail was picture book perfect. And it was. Satisfied but exhausted, she glanced in the mirror at the end of the hallway. Every speck of dirt she'd cleaned from the house was clinging to her. She'd become a human dust magnet. Sometime during her labors, her braid had come undone, and lint stuck to the escaping tendrils. Her once white shirt was now an indefinable shade of gray. The knees of her khaki trousers were as black as the circles under her eyes.

She probably shouldn't have told the cleaning crew to go home at midnight. There'd still been a lot of house left to polish up. But now it was done, and she could finally take a breather.

Jackie had never been so tired in her whole life. Maybe if she just sat down for a few minutes and propped up her feet, she'd be a new woman, rested enough to give her friend Winnie the proper greeting she deserved. And she knew exactly where she wanted to rest. She walked to the study, and brushing off the seat of her pants, sat down beside Butter, who had already claimed the left side of the window seat as her own. She stroked the cat's head and fell asleep almost before her head hit the lemon yellow pillows.

FIFTEEN

"I need a better light level in here!"

"Where's my extension cord? This thing isn't long enough."

"Has anyone seen my twenty-eight millimeter lens? Don't tell me I left it back at the studio . . ."

The shouts of strangers at close quarters caused Jacki to jump to her feet in alarm.

"Oh dear, look what you've done now. I told you not to bother Jacki. Can't you see how tired she is?" Taking a break from scolding the photographers who seemed to be everywhere, Winifred Longmont spread her plump arms wide open. "Hello, Jacki. Come over here and give us a hug."

"Smile!" One of the photographers flashed a light in Jacki's face. She put her hand over her eyes as she stumbled into Winnie's waiting arms.

"It's so good to see you!" Returning her friend's warm embrace, Jacki looked around the room. "What's going on here? You've brought your own personal paparazzi?"

"Oh no, not mine, dear. Yours and Patrick's."

"Ours?"

"Sandra Dixon is here. You know, the reporter

from *Architecture Now,*"a young female photographer interrupted. "She says she needs to see Patrick."

"That magazine is here?" Jacki asked.

"Well, of course, dear. Hadn't you heard? We're finalists for the Mitchell Burrell Medallion of Excellence. I haven't been this excited since I sat by Tom Selleck on an airplane to Hawaii." Winnie turned to the photographer. "Please tell Ms. Dixon that he's out by the reflecting pool. Patrick, not Tom Selleck, that is," she chuckled.

"We're finalists?" Jacki's voice rose in surprise. She didn't even know they'd entered the competition. Surely Patrick would have told her something that important. Maybe he'd just been so busy he forgot about it.

"Yes, of course you and Patrick are finalists. And I'm so proud I could pop. I knew you could do it. I could tell you'd be quite a team. My two award winners." Winnie gave her another bone-crushing hug. "Let's go see Patrick and hear what he has to say."

Jacki was suddenly very interested in what he might have to say, too.

Stepping over extension cords and dodging high-intensity lights, they arrived at the reflecting pool at almost the same time as the writer from the architectural journal. Sandra Dixon, a petite woman with a cloud of golden curls, took a microtape recorder out of her briefcase and laid it on a small patio table. "Hello, Mr. Godwin," she said in a soft, southern drawl that Jacki had to strain to hear. "My name is Sandra Dixon, and I'm here to do a story on the medallion finalists."

Jacki noticed that Patrick showed no surprise at

the reporter's statement. When had he found out? What else wasn't he telling her? She edged closer.

Patrick gave Sandra his trademark smile. When she fluttered her eyelashes back at him, Jacki felt like shoving them both into the reflecting pool, even though the probability of them drowning in a foot of water was highly unlikely.

As Sandra inched even closer to him, Jacki noticed that Patrick's smile got brighter, if that was possible. When they sat down side by side on the decorative bench and Sandra adjusted her skirt to give an optimal view of her shapely thigh, Jacki clenched her fists.

Maybe he wouldn't notice, she thought. But as he ran his finger under the edge of his collar, she knew darned well he did. The glow on his face almost matched his brightly colored tie.

His tie? Why was he wearing a tie? He hadn't worn a tie since his first day in Phoenix. Patrick had to have known about this photo shoot, and he hadn't even had the decency to warn her so she'd be presentable, too. Looking down at her filthy khakis, she tried to rub some of the dirt out of the knees. It was no good. She decided to save her energy until after the interview, when she could show Patrick exactly what she thought of his poor communication skills.

"Your wife must be very proud of your work." Sandra put her hand on his knee. "This design is so . . . clever." Jacki could have spotted this fishing expedition a mile away. The reporter's question was so obvious. Patrick had to see that.

Apparently, he was blinded by his sixty seconds of fame. "Oh, I'm not married." Giving a little laugh, he tugged on his tie.

Jacki hoped he was suffocating. Slowly.

Sandra patted his knee. "How unfortunate. I'm sure all the women in Maine must be lining up to congratulate you." She leaned forward and gave him a glimpse down the V-neck of her dress.

He raised his eyebrow. "Oh, well, I haven't spent much time in Maine since this project began. In fact, my office staff hardly knows me anymore." Sandra laughed at his attempt at humor.

She pulled a folder out of her bag. "Well, with all of those government projects your firm has snapped up in the last few weeks, I'm sure they'll see plenty of you for the next couple of years."

Jacki's stomach took a dive.

"New work?" he croaked. For once, Patrick seemed almost speechless.

Flipping open her folder, Sandra handed him a sheet of paper. "Yes, of course, silly. Don't be so modest." She pointed to an item on the paper. "The mayor's office faxed me this memo last night. You're under contract to design a new library and civic center for Portland, and a federal building, too. Those are plum assignments for a new firm."

After all they'd been through and all they'd done together, Patrick was leaving? And he'd known all along. In her haste to leave, Jacki tripped over an electrical cord. As the light it was attached to crashed to the ground and the bulb shattered with her heart, she felt like an utter fool. He'd lied to her. Their whole relationship was based on lies. What else had he lied about?

"Jacki, where are you going?" Winnie called out after her.

The sound of the crash and Winnie's voice ripped Patrick's attention away from the interview. What was going on?

He felt a hand on his shoulder. "Honey, we really do need to finish this interview. Let the techs clean up the mess. I'm sure they brought extra lights. They'll take care of it."

"It's not the lights I'm worried about." Patrick rose to his feet. "Please excuse me. Ms. Longmont can answer any other questions you have."

He took off in the direction Jacki had run. "Jacki!" he yelled, following her as quickly as he could through the maze of people and equipment. "Jacki! Wait! Is something the matter?"

But as he reached the front doors, the only evidence of Jacki was the dust billowing from behind her car as she raced down the road from Winnie's glorious new house.

For the first time in his life, Patrick didn't know what to do. He'd just left his seventeenth message on Jacki's machine. He'd been to the house four different times, but she wasn't there. She wasn't at the office, either. No one seemed to know where she was. Not even Mia.

Once he was sure that the crowd had left Winnie's, he went back to her house to see if she knew why Jacki had left in such a hurry.

"More cocoa?" Winnie offered as the two of them sat at her dining room table.

Patrick shook his head. "I just don't get it. Why was Jacki so upset? Was it that reporter?"

"That certainly didn't help, now did it?"

"I was just being polite to the media."

"Patrick, my boy, you have no idea what effect you have on the opposite sex, do you?"

"Well . . . I just like women. I didn't mean anything. Jacki should have known that. She's yelled at me about it enough."

"Then do you really think Jacki would get that upset because of a meaningless flirtation?" Winnie picked up the bone china teapot and refilled his cup anyway. "After all, you say she knows you."

"I thought she knew how I felt about her." He began to stir his drink over and over. "I told her I love her . . ." His voice trailed off as he realized he was back to his old habits.

Winnie snapped her shortbread cookie in half. "And you showed her how much you loved her by crushing her dreams."

"Crushing her what? How did I do that?" He ran his hands through his hair and waited for her answer.

"You blindsided her. Anyone could see that."

"I can't." He shook his head. "I really don't know what I did wrong, Winnie."

"Okay, then I'll tell you." Winnie reached for another cookie. "You told her you love her. Right?"

"Right. And that I was going to stay here." Patrick smacked his forehead with the palm of his hand as realization sank in. "Dumb. Really dumb."

"You bet it was, dear. And then, in front of a crowd of people, you let the reporter go on and on about your new projects on the other side of the country that will keep you busy and away from her for who knows how long."

Patrick shook his head sadly. "No wonder she hates me."

Winnie dunked her cookie in her cocoa. "No wonder."

Three weeks had passed since the last time Patrick had tried to contact Jacki. He must have left a hundred messages on her voice mail. Suddenly, they'd stopped. And now it looked as though her biggest fear—that he'd gone back to Maine for good—had been realized.

Jacki sat in her office wondering how she could have misjudged him so badly. Maybe her first impression of him had been the right one, after all.

The days went by in one big blur now that Patrick was gone. One day fused into the next. Jacki tried her best to fill the void created in her life with work. Lots of work. She was at her desk by five o'clock every morning, always before the sun rose.

She stayed at the job site of their newest project every day for at least three hours, determined that the Sage Inn Resort would be perfect, even if her personal life was in a shambles. Returning to the office, she'd work straight through until ten or eleven o'clock at night, leaving just as Curtis was finishing up.

The long hours of working seven days a week combined with the misery of losing Patrick started to take their toll on her. She began to look haggard, becoming painfully thin. Her even-tempered optimism turned into a cranky pessimism. For the first time since she was a child, she didn't attend the office

Christmas party. Even Mia tiptoed around her, afraid of causing an outburst over some minor infraction. Jacki was driving everyone hard, but she placed twice as many demands on herself.

Now it was New Year's Eve, and Mia had been insisting that Jacki go out with her and her friends to celebrate. In fact, Mia and Winnie still complained about her antisocial behavior at Christmas, how Jacki had opened her gifts in silence, then retreated to her room.

"Cuz, you've got to snap out of this." Mia's comment shook Jacki out of her depression for a moment.

"Snap out of what? I'm tired of all of you harassing me. Just leave me alone," Jacki responded tersely. She turned to the computer, pretending to study the figures on the screen in front of her.

"Listen up, grumpy. Stop thinking about yourself. For once, try to think of how your self-pity is affecting other people," Mia persisted. "Winnie is beside herself with worry. So am I."

Jacki turned around. Seeing the concern on her cousin's face, she began to feel a twinge of remorse. "Hey, I'll be okay. Honest. I'm sorry if I'm upsetting everyone. The holidays have been rough for me. I'll be fine when they're over. You and your friends go on to the New Year's Eve party. I'll just stay here a little longer, then I'll go home and celebrate with Bart."

"Do you want me to stay with you? How about Winnie? Do you want me to call her?" Mia stepped toward the door.

Jacki sighed. "No, you go on to your party. Bart

and I will be just fine. Really. I'm looking forward to spending New Year's Eve with a dog."

Mia scrutinized her Mickey Mouse watch. "Well, if you're sure you're not going with us, I'd better be on my way." She handed Jacki a torn piece of paper and kissed her on the cheek. "Here's the number of the place where the party's going to be. Call if you need me."

Mia started out of the office, then turned back. "Last chance."

Jacki shook her head. She got up and put her hands on Mia's shoulders, pushing her forward until they were in the lobby.

Mia stopped in her tracks. "Don't forget to—"

"Yes, yes, I know. I have the number right here. Get lost! And don't worry about me."

When Jacki returned to her office, she looked around at the decorations Mia had put all over it in a vain attempt to snap her out of her funk, and into a holiday mood. The credenza overflowed with brightly painted *nacimientos*—nativity scenes—of all shapes and sizes. Dozens of scarlet poinsettias lined the walls. A star-shaped piñata hung in one corner, and on the round oak table sat a small Christmas tree covered with dozens of tiny white lights and jammed full of more ornaments than she thought possible. Its pine scent permeated every corner of the room. Mia had plugged in the lights before she left, and they blinked merrily, as though mocking Jacki's foul mood.

It was nine o'clock. The strenuous work schedule Jacki had inflicted upon herself gave her an overwhelming urge to go home, crawl into bed and call it a night, New Year's Eve or no New Year's Eve. She decided to rest her head on her desk for a couple of minutes before she got back to work. Just as she began to lose her battle with fatigue, she heard something banging against a wall and knew, without a doubt, that she wasn't alone.

She stepped out of her office and walked down the hallway. Light poured from the open door of the storage room. Just then, a man stepped out.

Jacki found herself temporarily speechless. Patrick was supposed to be designing buildings in Maine, not standing in her hallway with a roll of duct tape dangling from one hand. She finally found her voice. "What are *you* doing here, Patrick?"

"I thought you'd be at the party. This was going to be a surprise. Did you know your door wasn't even locked? Anyone could get in."

"Anyone did get in," she reminded him.

Ignoring her comment, he closed the storage room door and, turning his back to her, began taping something to it.

"You didn't answer my question. Let's try it one more time. What are you doing here, Patrick?"

He faced her and stepped to one side. "This is what I'm doing here."

Jacki read the words on the paper aloud. "Godwin Architectural Associates, winner of the Mitchell Burrell Medallion of Excellence? You won? You really won?"

"No. *We* won. You and me. Your company and mine. And now that I'm relocating my firm, I need an office. I figure that I've done some of my best work in this room, so—"

"Relocating your firm?" She wasn't sure that she'd heard him correctly.

"Yes. We're an Arizona company now. But I also came to give you this." Reaching into his jacket pocket, he pulled out a long, satin-covered box from a well-known jeweler and held it out to her.

She pointedly rejected the offering. "Look, if you think you can force your way in here after almost three weeks of nothing—no phone calls, no letters, not even a damned postcard—and then try to bribe me into your bed with some piece of jewelry, some expensive bauble . . ."

"I did call you. Fifty-seven times, to be exact."

"Fifty-seven?" She raised an eyebrow in disbelief.

He nodded. "Not that anyone was keeping track. By the way, this isn't some piece of overpriced jewelry, and I'm not bribing you to go to bed with me. I'm not even offering to have sex with you again. Yet."

She crossed her arms in front of her. "Why would I even consider accepting a gift from you after you lied to me?"

"Lied to you?" His hand tightened around the rejected present. "How could I lie to you? You wouldn't even answer my phone calls. Fifty-seven of them. Remember? You have to actually have a conversation with someone before you can lie to them."

"Are you denying that you were going after new projects in Maine, even after you told me you were moving to Arizona for good?"

"Yes."

She raised her eyebrow in disbelief. "Then the Project Fairy just gave them to you as a gift?"

"Well, practically." He shrugged. "Derek and Ruth

went after those government projects because they were afraid they'd be out on the streets without them."

"And Derek and Ruth didn't tell you what they were doing? Your own employees didn't let you know about something that would have had such an enormous impact on your operations?"

"No. It was a surprise. A big one. Honest."

"So what are you going to do with the projects?"

"We declined two of them. But we couldn't get out of doing the library."

"Which means, of course, you're going back to Maine."

"Only one week out of every month. And when the library's finished, we relocate permanently to Arizona."

She still didn't know whether or not to trust him. "Can I have that in writing?"

He held the box out to her again. "Open this first."

Sighing, she took the gift from him and untied the gold ribbon. There, nestled inside, sat a pair of sterling silver chopsticks. So he'd felt it, too. Jacki's lips began to curve upward. Her eyes twinkled for the first time in a long time.

"Well, aren't you going to read them?"

Taking a chopstick out of the box with trembling fingers, she read softly, "We've only just begun. November seventh."

"That's the day I fell for you. Something about the way you eat tofu touched my heart . . . damn it, Jacki. You know I love you."

She held the chopsticks next to her heart.

"Will you marry me? I really do love you, Jacqueline Santiago. I've never needed anyone as much as I need you." Patrick waited uncertainly for her response.

"Yes, I think I just might do that. I felt like I was going to die when I thought you didn't love me, too." Jacki looped her arms around his neck. "Oh, and by the way, Patrick—it's going to be midnight in a couple of hours, and I need to warm up for my first kiss of the New Year."

Enthusiastically returning her embrace, Patrick was only too happy to oblige.

EPILOGUE

Three years later, Patrick sat cross-legged on the area rug in his living room, carefully setting the last alphabet block into place on the coffee table. The building was pretty impressive, even if he said so himself, and he'd used every alphabet block in the house to put it together. While he scooted back to admire his handiwork, fourteen-month-old Elena Winifred Godwin toddled over and plopped down on the floor between him and Bart.

He grinned at his brown-eyed, curly-haired daughter, noticing that she sat perfectly still as she stared at the structure he'd just created.

"Look, baby, Daddy's designed a building just for you. See this archway? Notice how I've added an extra column here for support?"

Patiently, she listened to him describe every architectural feature. Grabbing the sleeve of his shirt, the toddler pulled herself to her feet. She walked over to the coffee table. With one fell swoop of her arm, she destroyed his masterpiece, its destruction accompanied by gleeful baby chuckles.

"The women in my life. It looks as though I'll never be able to design anything to please them,"

Patrick grumbled. His smile contradicted his words, and it grew even larger as Jacki leaned over to give her husband a big, reassuring hug.

ABOUT THE AUTHOR

Deborah Shelley is the pen name of the writing team of Deborah Mazoyer and Shelley Mosley. They live in Glendale, Arizona, and have been writing together for five years. Deborah, a building safety manager, has a husband, Brian, and a daughter, Katie, who's seven. Shelley, a library manager, has a husband, David, a twenty-one year old son, Andrew, and an eighteen-year-old daughter, Jessica. Both Deborah and Shelley love humor, books, cats, romantic comedies, anything Disney, and, of course, chocolate.

They love to hear from their readers. You can reach them at:

DeborahShelley@inficad.com

or

P.O. Box 673
Glendale, AZ 85311